SKINDEEPMAGIC

skindeepmagic

SHORT FICTION

Craig Laurance Gidney

REBEL SATORI PRESS
Bar Harbor • New Orleans

Published in the United States of America by
REBEL SATORI PRESS
P.O. Box 363, Hulls Cove, ME 04644
www.rebelsatori.com

Conjuring Shadows appeared the online magazine *Expanded Horizons in November 2011*; Mauve's Quilt appeared in the anthology *Magic in the Mirrorstone*; The poem "Shadow" by Richard Bruce Nugent is from *Gay Rebel of the Harlem Renaissance: Selections from the work of Richard Bruce Nugent* by Thomas H. Wirth.

Book design by Sven Davisson
Cover Design by Thomas Drymon

Library of Congress Cataloging-in-Publication Data

Gidney, Craig Laurance, 1967-
 [Short stories. Selections]
 Skin deep magic : stories / By Craig Laurance Gidney.
     pages cm
 Includes bibliographical references and index.
 ISBN 978-1-60864-102-4 (pbk. : alk. paper)
 1. Magic--Fiction. 2. Fantasy fiction, American. 3. American fiction--African American authors. 4. Gays' writings, American. I. Title.
 PS3607.I275S55 2014
 813'.6--dc23
                    2014014271

Thanks to Jeffrey Burka, Christopher Herrmann, and Samuel Barkdull for the manuscript assistance. Thanks to Sven Davisson and Rebel Satori Press for publishing *Skin Deep Magic*.

To my family

My skin is black
My arms are long
My hair is woolly
My back is strong
Strong enough to take the pain
Inflicted again and again
—"Four Women," Nina Simone

Contents

Pyschometry, or Gone with the Dust

"She's a hoarder," says Philip. "Or, she was one."

I've seen that show on TV, where people collect and obsess over mountains of rubbish that decays. And *Grey Gardens* is one of my favorite movies; I've seen it at least a million times. That movie is like a real life Tennessee Williams play set in a decaying mansion. So, I'm prepared. Or at least I think I am. Possums, raccoons, and feral cats don't really bother me. But fecal matter, urine, rats, and roaches *do* scare me.

"Here we go," says Philip. And he opens the door to the late Agnes F's bungalow.

"Jesus X. Christ." I say that aloud; I say it two more times in my head.

It's not the stuff that overwhelms me—though there are mountain ranges of it from floor to ceiling. No. It's the smell. The Smell is ripe, rich, and relentless. It has layers, like the finest perfume: must, dust, mold, old paper, and of course, death. The fire marshal found Agnes F gently rotting among her beloved possessions. Rumor had it that she was smiling. The Smell is more than the sum of its parts. It assaults all my senses and deranges them. It swirls and eddies through the hillocks and valleys of junk like a sluggish river. I can see the Smell, rising and curling like cartoon stink lines. If it were a color, the Smell would be the grey-pink of raw organ meat. I swear I can hear the Smell slithering among the mounds.

"I'm gonna need a minute," I say.

Philip wrinkles his nose in sympathy. He reaches into his backpack, and says, "Thank God I bought these."

He hands me a face mask before putting his on.

The electricity is off, so we have to use our torches to find the

1

window shutters. As we move through the house, things crunch and crack. I feel no carpet or hardwood floor beneath me. I am grateful that I remembered to wear my shit-kicking hiking boots. (The first time I did this, I was wearing heels!) We finally reach the shutters, and open them, letting light flood into the dark, dank room. I open the windows, to air the room out a little.

"Jeez, Margo," says Philip. "Our Agnes was a bit of a collector. She certainly wasn't politically correct."

"What do you mean?" I turn around, and see for myself: "Oh."

They line the shelves and stare at us with their dead eyes, in frozen poses. The comical, inhuman stances. The dark fabric to represent skin, the tufts of wool to represent hair. They watch us as we walk in the room. These dark dolls and Negro memorabilia were Agnes F's prized possessions. I see pickaninny dolls, girls with plaited hair sticking out at all angles, and the boys munching on felt watermelons. There are mammies of all kinds, as cookie jars, posters, dolls and syrup bottles. And that's not all. The floor is full of all sorts of weird stuff. Candy wrappers, flour sacks, telephone bills, deeds, and canceled checks. In one corner, I see a lawn jockey poking out from bubble wrap.

"Maybe a house full of raccoons and feral cats would have been better," I say, an attempt at gallows humor.

"You know Jack, back at the home office?" says Philip, "He said he went to a house where the guy kept Nazi memorabilia. Teapots and commemorative plates and shit."

"Well, Agnes and that guy would've made a lovely couple."

"Yeah. Not that we'd be on the invite list—a fairy and a negress."

I flinch at the word *negress*. Philip means well. I just don't like that word, even if it is used 'ironically.' And here, in this context, it's just hella creepy. "Let's get started," I say, "I don't want to be here too long. My skin's crawling..."

We set up a couple of battery-powered lanterns to add to the natural sunlight. Philip begins pawing through the trash, and I start at the shelves. I take out my digital camera and start snapping pictures. I know that there's a market for this stuff on Ebay and other sites. One man's trash is another man's treasure, the saying goes. After a while, I settle into the rote repetition of the work, and the creep factor subsides.

I like this job. The macabre aspects (i.e., the sudden death of people, their squabbling or distraught long-lost relatives) aren't my favorite thing to deal with. But walking in someone's abandoned house is like entering their mind. It's like seeing the physical manifestations of their memories, and in some cases, their neuroses. I've found war bonds worth a lot of money and pillowcases full of cash. I've also found manuscripts of poetry and novels that never got published, most of them rubbish, but some of them quite good. And one time, in a house, I found a room full of weird, humanoid sculptures made out of bubble wrap and packing tape. They were about as tall as I am, these transparent, deformed people hidden away in an old man's guest room. But the thing I like most about cataloging dead people's estates are the stories that I can piece together.

Sometimes, when I touch things, like a ring or beloved toy, I can get impressions from them. Images, distant voices, smells. Sometimes, an entire story will unfold. I've never told anyone about this. It sounds too New Agey and silly. I can hear my mom saying, "Oh, Margo, you've always had such a *vivid* imagination." So I keep the impressions I get from things to myself.

The first thing I touch is a cookie jar , shaped as the head of a black mammy. The jar is cracked and faded. Her eyes are scratched out. She's been glued together so many times that the black glaze of her skin has white spots, as if she has vitiligo. Her wide lips are scraped, lending her smile a sinister aspect. I lift the lid off her head, and there's an empty space where her brains should be. Looking into it, I hear a faint voice of ceramic shards breaking.

My senses are flooded. Cookies fill my head: molasses and gingersnaps and snickerdoodles, and someone named Timmy's favorite, chocolate chip with pecan. The smell of spices and butter and chocolate fills my nostrils, as does the smell of dust and emptiness. I feel grubby hands on my face, wearing my ceramic skin down, fading my black, glossy color. The mammy jar tells me her story in shimmering mirages that fade quickly. One family who owned her gave her a name. Miss Betsy. Miss Betsy, who was warmth and love and sweetness. Another family used her to store nuts, bolts, and loose change. They called her the Niggerhead. As in, "S___, could you get me some quarters outta the niggerhead?" Miss Betsy sat in bright kitchens and then, when she was no longer fashionable, in dark garages and flea market tables.

I put Miss Betsy aside.

I pick up a strange looking doll that looks like a Raggedy Andy dipped in tar. The hair is rough and prickly, and the lips are the color of watermelon and take over half its face, while the eyes were wide saucers. The doll mingles the horrific and the humorous simultaneously. These are golliwogs, British versions of pickaninnies. Agnes F sure loved her Negro memorabilia; her collection is international.

"Who loved you, baby?" I say under my breath, holding the pitiful creature. A twisted child's story plays before my eyes:

The blackest imp spends most of his time in the corner of the blackest cave. Of course, it's a mess. It's filthy and musty, full of brown moss, the carcasses of crickets, old fish bones and porn magazines full of naked fairy girls. The cave goes half a league underground. Tubers and the frayed threads of roots glow in the light of his fiery eyes. A few baubles and treasures are strewn here and there: a half read book, a dusty kaleidoscope, a bit of cobalt glass. He never has time to clean or organize his treasures. Who does he hate the most? The eternally young elves; his mother and father, who gave him life and these cursed genes; and the fairyland that wishes that he would hide away.

He hears a group of giggling fairies and young elf bucks talking outside of his cave.

One of the males says, "I hear that he's horrible looking."

A fairy princess replies: "I've heard the same thing. But I still feel sorry for it."

"You shouldn't," says the alpha-elf. "There's a natural order to things, Buttercup. If he were out here, he would hurt you, without remorse. Those golliwogs are savages."

Malevolence stirs in the desiccated prune of his heart. His gaze turns all into cinders. He longs to punch the elf, and rend him. He wants to rip the filigree wings off the stupid fairy princess. Let them talk that way about him, then!

He just stews in his hatred in the back of the cave. Soon, he will make his move. Then, he will have a heart as black as his skin.

I drop the horrid thing on the floor, stung by its hatred and bitterness.

I move away, done with the dolls and their tales of quiet desperation.

Hours later, full of ironic banter and the occasional horror (an ant colony found in one room, and the fridge full of decaying food and mold spores) we uncover Agnes F's *piece de resistance*: a lawn jockey.

The statue is in great disrepair. The flesh, what's left of it, is covered in rust that looks like age spots. The lantern is missing, leaving an extended hand holding nothing. How much would this go on eBay?

"These were on the front lawns where I grew up," says Philip. I can't figure out his mood. Is he wistful? Or embarrassed?

I examine the figure closely.

"It looks like someone messed with it. Look here. It looks like it was modified. Who would do that?"

Against my better judgment, I touch the thing, and let it give me its story.

Brady looked at the finished product. It was awesome! It was size of that black midget actor with the famous catchphrase. The paint job was fresh, metallic. His little vest shone, the same color as his blood-red lips, and his cap was white and clean, like his pants. The eyes fluttered, and there was the whir of animatronics as the circuitry settled.

Brady pressed the remote control, and it stood up. There was an oversized clock around its neck, like that rapper who was in a reality dating show. He giggled. He'd sampled the rapper's famous catchphrase, so when the robot won the battle, it would say "Yeah, boyeee!" The arm that held the lantern was retrofitted with a buzz saw that could cut the metal of the other robots. The other arm had a gleaming blade of surgical steel his dad had made him. Both blade and buzz saw had been tested on abandoned car parts and cutlery that his friends bought him.

"Jeez, that's cool." Hunter had walked up behind him. Brady hadn't heard him come in. "What're you going to call him?"

"I dunno. I was thinking RoboGangsta."

Hunter laughed. "How about L'il Killah."

"Or Fo' Shizzle."

"Word."

Both boys burst out laughing, and flashed gang symbols to each other.

When they recovered, Brady said, "L'il Killah will make the other robots its bitch."

"You wanna test it out on something? Mom's got an old vacuum cleaner in the garage that's going to the junk heap."

Brady responded by pressing a couple of buttons on the remote control. The buzz saw spun, and L'il Killah said, "Yeah, boyeee!"

"Margo? Are you OK?"

I step back from the lawn jockey. It's more like a stagger. Philip has to catch me before I crash land on a pile of garbage. That last vision was the most intense one I've had, ever. I felt those boys' glee, heard the hip-hop they had on their iPods. I knew the websites where they got the schematics for their robots, and the television shows they liked.

"I think it's the fumes," I say.

Philip says, "I've gotten quite used to it—the Eau d'Agnes."

I laugh, weakly.

"Why don't you step outside and get some fresh air? We'll go to lunch, soon."

I nod at him, thinking that lunch is the last thing I want.

Outside, the air is humid and thick as soup, but it's still better than being inside that sad woman's home. There were ghosts in that room. And they weren't the flimsy, will-o-the-wisp things, either. No. These were strong spirits that lived in the objects. And every object I handled was a potential trap.

"Margo, can you come inside? I need your help with something," says Philip.

"Be there in a moment."

I prepare mentally myself to go back in there, that house of dust, death, and secret histories.

What story will emerge from the next thing I touch?

Sapling

Dryad Park was on the other side of Nix Street, the safest street to walk home on. Bodegas that overcharged lined the street, along with houses overflowing with kids and a liquor store. Old potato chip bags blew along the street in the autumn breeze, mingling with leaves and gum wrappers. It wasn't quite twilight, but the woods were dark. Mabel heard that things went on in there. Drug deals, gay hookups, and rapes. She would have ignored it, passed right by it. After all, it wasn't just her mother who avoided Dryad Park. Anyone with sense did. But she saw a man walking into the park, and he wasn't an ordinary man.

For one thing, there was what he wore. He was in a dark green shirt that was as long as a dress. It was embroidered with white, and white designs snaked around the shirt. His pants were black, and he wore sandals, even though it was beginning to get chilly in the evenings. The man's hair was dreadlocked, two thick matted braids. Little shell earrings hung from the larger shells of his ears. He had bark-brown skin. Before he entered the wood, he turned around, and caught her eye. His own eyes flashed at her, like cats'. He turned, a shape of green and black against the yellow of the leaves and the brown of the trunks.

Mabel stood still for a while. She glanced around her. She saw a chubby brown toddler staring at her from his porch. Had he seen the strange man? Without thinking, she walked across the street, and stood at the edge of park. She paused. Her mother's warnings loomed in the back of her mind. The man was probably going into the park for a drug deal, or maybe to have sex. She found both prospects revolting and thrilling at the same time. She glanced into the park, and tried to peel away the layers of twilight and leaves and mulch to see him. But he had vanished.

SAPLING

The next day, Mabel saw two men enter the park. One was Latino, with long hair, teeth lined with gold, and wore a t-shirt that had a clown with fangs. The other was black, had his hair in thick prison braids, and wore a t-shirt with the Tasmanian Devil. Both frowned as they entered the park. One of them, Clownshirt, turned and saw her staring at them. He smiled at her threateningly. Gold teeth daggers flashed. Mabel averted her gaze quickly, and went into the bodega.

She moved through the aisles of exotic fruits and Saran-wrapped baked goods until she came to the aisle of strange sodas and juices. Guava, coconut, and mango juices were in ribbed white cans with Spanish written on them. She picked a new drink, Guarana, and slipped it into her back pack. She didn't have any money, but she didn't need any. The old storekeeper never seemed to see her. She looked at the oval fun house mirror that reflected the refrigerated section. She didn't see herself.

When she came out of the bodega, the two men were out of sight. She was relieved; and she felt stupid. Did she really think that she'd see that man in green again? She sipped her soda. The tanginess hit her, and the carbonation lightly burned her throat. Her mother would be back from the store soon. Soda was on her list of bad things, so she had to finish it soon.

Mabel gulped it down, and started to head home. She saw the man in the corner of her eye. He now wore a filmy shirt the color of green apples. His pants were dark, and he wore delicate lime-green slippers. He glided down Nix Street, and dipped into the forest.

"No, don't!" The words were out of Mabel's mouth before she knew it. Mabel dropped her empty can, and darted across the street. It was too dangerous for the man to go into the park, but he was already down the slope. Mabel hovered on the edge. Evening bloomed, and streetlight ignited. The man was so beautiful. He was swallowed by woods and the darkness. Mabel saw the green glow of his shirt against the gathering dusk. She hoped that he would be safe from the two rough looking guys who'd entered. But what could she do? Mabel headed home.

It was like pushing through a spider's web. He'd moved through layers of time, always pushing the tickling strands out of his face. It had clung to him, with feather-soft touches. He moved through the perpetual gloaming until he emerged where it was grey, but clear of the mesh that surrounded his journey. Here, he was in a forest of some kind, but it was much noisier than the forest where he came from. He remembered that, from his visits here before. Technology was never far off. Even now, in the twilight, you couldn't see the stars; they were obscured by the orange glow of the city nearby. He had heard the scrape and whine of vehicles, and smelled food, urine, garbage and animal droppings. All were bound together with a chemical odor. Even the air tasted sour. He hated this place, yet he had to be here.

Now, back in the park, he moved away from the slope where forest ended and the concrete world began. It was time to replenish himself.

"Hey, where you going?"

He turned to face the speaker. He saw two men, one dark and one brown, advance on him. Both had cigarettes dangling from their mouths. Both casually blocked his way. Both wore shirts emblazoned with demons, the dark man with an animal of some kind, the lighter one with the face of a man made up to look sinister. The word 'clown' drifted up from his memories.

It had been years since he used his voice. It came out in a croak. English was a harsh language. "I am going to my—home."

"Naw you ain't," said Clownshirt. He smiled.

Devilshirt spat, laughed, and replaced his cigarette.

Clownshirt said, "You came in here to get your dick sucked."

"Look like a damn woman," mumbled Devilshirt.

The suppressed violence simmered in the air. He could see it blister the air around the two of them like a heat image. He could taste their evil.

"Maybe you want to suck *our* dicks," said Clownshirt. He grabbed his crotch suggestively. Devilshirt reached in his pocket, produced a blade. He could smell the old blood that it had spilled.

He had to stop this before it went any further.

He pulled the air around him and buried himself in it.

"Hey, where'd he go?"

"That faggot up and disappeared. Shit!"

He moved in the bubble of dark air until he reached the street. It was slow going, like walking in a heavy cloak that wanted to burst apart.

The street was ugly, as all things in this world were. It was a scar on the earth, filled in with black tar like old blood. The rich palate of color of a natural twilight with its silvers, grays, mauves and greens, was obscured by lamplight and car light and neon light into a smear of orange-brown. Concrete pressed down on the earth, and confined it. Along the street, garbage swirled in wind eddies along with leaves. He removed the dark bubble. Two glowing eyes—headlights—plowed toward him, screamed away.

The driver cursed, called him a freak. After he crossed the river of black tar, he remembered what he needed in this world. What he wore would never do. He would have to change much about himself. The way he walked, how he dressed. He would need a name.

The clothes part he could deal with easily. He cast a glamour on himself, where most people would see him as a normal, nonthreatening man in unremarkable clothes. It beat having to actually *wear* the confining garments! People here would probably see him as a middle-aged brown man in jeans and a button-down shirt. He recalled his name—Jack. It sounded strange.

He tasted the wind. The girl had been here recently. Where did she live? He followed her scent.

Her mother started in on her the moment she walked into the apartment.

"You're late."

"Only by five minutes."

"I don't want you walking the street after dark, you hear me?"

"But it gets dark early. I can't help it."

"Girl! Don't give me anymore lip. You are to be home when I say so. Or, I'll have to come and pick you up after school. Do you want that?"

Mabel was mortified. She could just see her mother picking her up at school, while all of the other kids watched. The silence was her answer.

She moved to the coffee table and took out her books. She started working on algebra while Mom bustled around the kitchen, finishing dinner. At 7:30, Mom called her to the dining room table. They bowed their heads, and Mom began one of her endless prayers. It was full of thy's and thou's. "And Lord, I especially want you to look after my daughter, and guide her well. Keep her safe from the wickedness of the world..."

Mom began to follow Sister Vivian about three years ago. Mabel thought the reason for this sudden devotion was after Mabel's illness, but she wasn't sure. Three years ago was a blur. She was told she was in a coma for a while. Mabel just remembered that the world was out of focus, then. Colors, shapes, sounds and smells were all the same, a kaleidoscopic smear that she couldn't distinguish. Everything had an aura around it that burned their shapes away. When she woke up from that endless fever dream, a month had passed by, and Mom was suddenly religious, in a scary kind of way.

Sister Vivian appeared Sundays on the public access channel. Her mother knelt in front of the TV, transfixed by a homely woman in a white nun's outfit. Sister Vivian had a medium brown complexion with a pebbly skinned texture. She was maybe three hundred pounds, and her white gown barely covered her immensity. She was always against a background of deep blue sky strewn with clouds. It looked like she was floating. Sister Vivian would begin by reading a Bible verse in the old-fashioned language. Actually, it was more like singing than reading. There was an operatic timbre to her thou's and thy's. When she would explain what the verse meant, the most marvelous transformation took place. Her eyes would bug out. Her crinkled flesh would crinkle even more, as she growled out her observations and insights in a guttural bass voice. She looked like Jabba the Hut, and sounded like him, too. Each and every sentence was punctuated with a "hurr-ah."

("And Jesus died on the cross for you, hurr-ah. He was whipped and nailed and tortured for our sins, so we might enter the Kingdom of Heaven, hurr-ah!")

The first time she saw the floating Jabba woman, Mabel laughed. That was a mistake. Mom warned her never to laugh at Sister Vivian. Indeed, it was Sister Vivian's prayers that had brought Mabel back from the brink of death.

After dinner, Mabel finished her homework. She put on the TV while her mother sat across from her, reading the latest Sister Vivian pamphlet. The thin paper was tattered and filled with her mother's notes and underlines. Mom was focused on reading the pamphlet for the millionth time. Keeping an eye on her, Mabel changed the channel. She had been watching a mother-approved show, a nature program about meerkats. She turned to a banned program, about single black women in New York City.

One of them said something off-color about men on the Down Low. Mabel laughed.

Mom looked up, and glanced at the television. Moments like these were terrifying. Despite doing it for the past year, she always thought it would fail.

"Those critters are cute," her mother said. She smiled at Mabel, and went back to studying her pamphlet. Mabel let go of the breath she'd held.

It was in January when she realized that had some sort of *power*. It wasn't magic, not exactly. When Mabel thought of magic, she thought of wizards and talking owls and wands. It was more about not being noticed. She and her mother were clothes shopping, and Mom kept on buying clothes that were too young for her. Skirts with flowers, barrettes that sparkled. When she found some jeans with rhinestones outlining the pockets, Mom said no.

"They make you look older than you are. No way, baby."

"Everyone is wearing them. They're not—miniskirts."

"They're hip-huggers. No, Mabel. I said no. Let's move on."

They weren't hip-huggers. Not exactly, anyway. Mabel took the jeans, pouting. She carried them around the store. When Mom looked back at her, and showed her new clothes, she made no mention of the rhinestone jeans she was carrying. Mabel thought it was odd. She put the jeans in the cart cautiously. When they went to check out, and unloaded the little girl clothes on the cashier's counter, Mom didn't say a word. Mabel kept waiting for Mom to throw a hissy fit, but the cashier rung the jeans up with the rest of their order. When they got home, Mabel took the jeans to her room. She touched them, felt the texture of denim and the blunted sharpness of the rhinestones. She couldn't believe that they were real. Had her mother changed her mind, and just not told her? That didn't seem likely.

Sister Vivian's latest series of programs had been about the wantonness of today's youth, a new generation of "Jezebels." It was more likely that this was a trap, and Mom would yell at her for trying to trick her. But this seemed unlikely, too. Mom was frugal; she would never spend fifty-eight dollars on a lesson when a simple no would do. She didn't wear the rhinestone jeans for months.

It was spring when Mabel got the courage to wear them. Looking in the mirror, noticing how they conformed to her new curves, Mabel had to grudgingly admit that they were hip-huggers. She stepped out of her room that morning cautiously. Her mother sat at the kitchen table, reading the Bible verse for the day. Mabel grabbed her book bag and moved toward the door.

"Hey. Ain't you gonna say goodbye?"

Mabel froze. She could feel the ax poised above her, ready to fall and slice her rhinestone hip-huggers into ribbons. She turned around slowly.

She gasped.

Mom's eyes were clouded. Her brown eyes had specks of gray in them. They moved across the planet of her eyes like an asteroid belt. The tiny black orbs in the center of the maroon sea were pinpricks.

"Goodbye..."

Mom's head fell to the page in front of her. The gray specks remained, and glittered like rhinestones.

Mabel finished her homework after dinner and got ready for bed.

Mom was still pissed about her being five minutes late. "I was going to let you have some ice cream, but since you didn't follow my rules... Look, baby, I know that I may seem too hard on you, but you'll understand, when you're a mother."

Mabel was brushing her teeth. Mom was watching her, like she was a little kid. She deliberately used a lot of toothpaste, so that she was foaming like a rabid dog. This did not deter Mom's lecture.

Mabel walked to her room in a fog of sullenness. She hoped that Mom could feel the tendrils of it. But Sister Vivian's righteous words blinded her. Mabel flopped down on the bed.

"Don't forget to say your prayers!"

She got out of bed, and knelt.

"Dear God, please watch over me and my mother, so that we might be safe." She opened her eyes a crack. Her mother's shadow fell on the bed. "And please, Lord, keep my father safe, wherever he is..."

The silhouette of her mother's shadow withdrew quickly. Mabel smiled.

The forest is singing. To her. Its voice is deep, deeper than Sister Vivians' when she goes into a trance. Mabel finds herself in its midst. The trees are the legs of black men, with afros of green that rise up to the sky. The sky is

dark denim blue, decorated with rhinestone stars. The forest is huge and dark and mysterious. It is far from the road; Mabel can't even hear cars in the distance, or children crying or ambulances. No, there's just the voice of the forest, and the world is muffled in green darkness. She should be afraid, but she's not. She feels—safe.

Mabel moves forward, but she doesn't go far. The air weighs on her. Each step is as slow as if she's walking underwater. Half seen images move at the corner of her eyes, then disappear. Faces, animals, and other things. The night is full of eyes. Somehow, she knows that they can't hurt her.

The song draws her on.

The song, which was also a scent, led him to an apartment building not too far from the park. He stared at it for a while, hidden in a bubble of air. The concrete steps were cracked and brown grass crumbled and died in the wounds. A broken window had black tape holding the shards together. Each window had a metal box hanging from it. The street in front of the building was full of plastic bottles and had trash floating in it.

So this is where my daughter lives.

He didn't know how long he had stood across the street, watching the abomination of concrete, tar, glass and metal. Car fumes, the chemical tang of perfume, deodorant, fluorocarbons and household cleansers all swirled in his nose, went down to his lungs, and made him sick. Even the sun here was different, filtered through ozone holes and the exhaust of the city. It was a dirty sun, debased by these things, this miasma of artificiality. His stomach began to grumble, and he felt bile rising up like a tide. He began to retch, and a thin, whitish liquid slipped out of his nose and mouth. It burned his throat.

When he was finished being sick, he glanced up quickly, worried that he was exposed. But the bubble of air was still in place. It wouldn't be for long. He would have to leave soon and regain his strength. This world was making him ill. He began to walk back to the park, when someone tripped over him.

It was a woman carrying groceries. The brown paper bag slipped from her grasp and jars and eggs hit the pavement. He grabbed her arm before she fell.

She didn't seem to notice that an invisible hand was steadying her. Her eyes were on the ground, following the trail of broken jars and eggs. She cursed. He recognized the voice. It had the dusky, husky sound that he remembered.

Cerise Green.

As Cerise began to salvage her groceries, he remembered when she wasn't so old, withered by the poison of this world. Yes, through the webbing of wrinkles, he could still see her youthful, smooth skin, brown as bark.

It was years ago, when she came to the forest. Her skin was ashen, her hair brutally short. Her lips were as cracked as the sidewalks were now, her arms covered in needle pricks. Her odor was off, unwashed body and chemical taint. Something coursed in her veins, an elixir of some kind, that changed her cells. Visions sprang out of her wildly, and stained the air. He saw that she was on fire and she watched the world melt around her. She was terrified of the green darkness, even as she sought it out to hide in. The smell of fear was rank on her. He heard the snapping twigs on the ground, and she looked about nervously before she darted, rabbit-quick, deeper into the woods.

He was tree-shaped then, drinking golden sunlight. Two men ran by him. They were sheened with sweat, and stank of violence. This was what spurred him to action, that and the girl's fear. Man-shaped, he had to get used to walking again, to limbs and blood and mucus and sweat. He was clumsy, as he followed the trio through the woods. The physicality of things hindered him. But they were noisy in their travels, and there wasn't a place in the forest that he didn't know.

He found them shortly. One of the men held the girl by the arm. The other one slapped her across the face and called her a bitch. She screamed, and was punched in the face for the effort. Bright blood coated her teeth, and frothed out in spit. The man holding her twisted her shoulder. Her pain, fueled by the chemical in her veins, created visions in front of her in shades of blue ice and violet fire.

He found his voice. It had been eons since he spoke. Stop, he said.

He must have looked horrifying, a thing not quite man and not quite tree. Twigs for fingers, birds in the vines of his hair, dripping moss, sloughing bark, growing flesh. Ruined berries that hardened into eyes, whorls into mouth and nostrils. He saw their horror. The man who had slapped the girl began to cry. The other one soiled himself and let go of the girl, who was lost in her blue and violet world of terror. His voice, he knew, was the voice of oak, tinged with acid green. As they left, he touched the girl, and moved her to a pocket of time that was peaceful.

She fell asleep.

He became more man, less tree.

He washed the blood from her face, found curative herbs, and healed her. He sang the poison out of her veins, and cleared the ash from her face. The blue and violet fire burned itself out.

She slept soundly as green darkness turned to green light.

She woke once, and saw his face. He was finished becoming a man, mostly. His blood was still sap-thick and sluggish.

By the light of the moon, her brown eyes sparkled. "Jesus," she said, and fell back asleep, finally free of fear and pain.

"Jesus, forgive me," Cerise said now, gathering her things, salvaging what she could. He stood as still as a tree, watching her. She walked across the street to the cage of concrete and metal.

"Beware the heathen," boomed Sister Vivian from the television. The impossible blue sky that served as her backdrop never changed. Her wimple was askew, and sweat poured down her face. Mabel could see the reflection of klieg lights on her dark skin. "The devil comes to us in many guises, to lead us from the path of righteousness. He is seductive, hurr-ah! He is deceitful, hurr-ah! His tongue is filled with honeyed lies, hurr-ah! ..."

"Yes," said her mother. Her head was bowed, and a hand raised and waving, as if Sister Viv could see her through the screen. Mabel knew that her mother was thinking about her father. Her mother never spoke of him. "Please, baby, don't ask me about him. I made some terrible choices when I was younger. I don't want to revisit them..."

Mabel had enough of Sister Vivian. Outside it was beautiful. Why was she stuck inside? The sunlight poured through the curtains, and she could see a slice of sky that was cloudless and pure blue. She stood up, and left her mother in a vacuum, full of Sister Vivian's ecstasies and wisdom. It was like shaping air and thought and sound into glass. Her mother sat in a snow globe, safe from the world. Tears began to spill out of her mother's eyes, as she relived her former life, the one with Mabel's father. She left the apartment.

Mabel walked toward the commercial district without any real goal. The side streets were mostly empty, with a Sunday morning hush. Every now and then she would see women in their Sunday best. Black women in solid colors and heels, crowned with hats, heading towards storefront churches, or women from El Salvador in floral dresses around the fronts of the Iglesias. Each group seemed happy, as they gossiped and shared stories with each other. She felt a pang of envy. Past the street of churches, the commercial district appeared. The sidewalks were lined with street merchants that sold DVDs, books, hats, gloves and knock off designer handbags and perfumes. The stores were mostly fast food restaurants, a couple of clothes retailers, and one antique shop. Mabel dipped into the musty shop, drawn in by the display of Tiffany lamps in the window. She wandered down overstuffed aisles, filled with old cadenzas, music boxes, dishes and cocktail glasses. Across from the cashier, there was a shelf filled with glass figurines. Paperweights with petrified bolts of color, swans and unicorns of cut crystal.

The glass tree, though, took her breath away. It was tiny, but she could see each wrinkle in the bark, which was tinted amber. The boughs and branches spread out, with leaves of green glass. Tiny berries of brilliant red were hidden among branches and leaves. The tree was about the size of her balled fist, but it drained the light of the store, absorbed it. It was the brightest figure on the shelf, and stole the unicorn and the swan's prisms.

It was an animal instinct that drove her. She had to have the glass tree. She had no money, and did not know where she would hide the treasure. But that didn't matter in the least. The desire burned in her. Her fingers tingled.

They will not see me. You will not see me.

The clerk was looking right at her, as he straightened the counter. He had three rotten teeth, his hair was lank and greasy, and what beauty he once had was smashed out of him by life, cigarettes and drugs. He looked right at her, but he didn't see her. Mabel looked into his dark, booze-reddened eyes, searched for her reflection. She only saw a swan and a unicorn dancing their depths.

She snatched the glass tree. Electricity was in her hand. She pulsed with green, amber and red. She was glass and bark and Mabel. She was unseen and her blood sang with sap and shards of glass. She walked out of the store, into the autumn sunlight, holding autumn sunlight in her hands.

She walked down the street. The sunlight was different, somehow. It had a form, a shape. It was a wave of rich yellow that spilled against the air that held a million sparkles. It looked like lemonade. She stuck out her tongue, and tasted the flowing invisible liquid.

It was warm and sweet, like honey. Energy coursed through her veins as she drank down the golden shimmer. She drank down the sky and searched for the earth hidden beneath the concrete. She also tasted the foul smells that hung in the air, dissonant notes of spoiled and rotten things that tainted the liquid energy. She could drink forever, but she stopped. It wasn't a pure taste of sunlight.

Mabel hurried home, feeling sudden guilt at putting her mother in that space with Sister Vivian. No-one deserved that. She moved through the press of people. On one of the tables of DVDs, she saw a couple of movies that she'd wanted to watch. She snatched them.

They can't see me!

She laughed, as she fingered the glass tree in her pocket.

That was when she saw *it*.

It was a whirlwind in the air. The lemonade sunlight flowed to the spinning thickness in the air that pulsed like a translucent heart. The bubble hid something, like her own bubble hid her. She dropped the stolen DVDs.

If she stared long enough, layers of invisibility flaked off the whirlwind heart, like dead skin. She saw him, a vague outline in glycerin. The man from the park.

Mabel ran, falling out of her bubble into real world. Voices and sounds came back to her with force. She smashed into an old church lady, who screeched in indignation. Mabel ignored her.

Watching Mabel run away from him broke his heart. He wanted to go up to her, and tell her who he was. Don't be afraid, he'd tell her. His branches ached to hold her. But he would have to move carefully, and be delicate about it. She was changing, growing into her power. He saw that Mabel was enjoying some of her abilities. But she would soon learn that there was another side to it all. Like all things, it came with price.

Jack began to feel ill again. He would soon have to go back into the forest and replenish himself. When he was stronger, he would make contact with her.

As he moved through the world of concrete and chemicals, he remembered the second time he'd seen Cerise. Time had passed in the human world, weeks or even months when she came back to the park. He was healing his stationary brothers and sisters, soothing them as they absorbed the poisoned air and tainted sunlight of this world. He was

21

also waiting for Cerise. She stirred things in him, things he had never felt in his long life. Her youth, her energy, and, frankly, her beautiful brown skin enticed him. The smell of flesh was different than the smell of bark and sap. It was sweet, copper and salt. Flesh was soft, as tender as the earth after a soaking rain. When she re-entered the wood, he could feel it. The doe-soft tentativeness of her walk traveled through the earth in gentle reverberations. The air around her smelled fresh, and she was free of the poison in her veins. Jack led her to him, through messages he sent to his brothers and sisters. Bushes and trees, even mosses gave Cerise subtle signals that guided her to him.

When she stepped into the clearing, he saw that she was changed. Her skin was new, and her hair was soft. She wore a white sweater and blue jeans. She had gained weight, and her body curved like the world. She was looking for him, he knew. She was looking for "Jesus." When she saw him waiting for her, he was ready.

His hair was thick and knotted into locks, and he had a beard. The tinge of green was almost imperceptible, and his skin was smooth and dark as mud. He'd practiced being completely human.

They stared at each for a while, both dappled by Jack's siblings. Finally, she said, "I just had to make sure that you were real...I...I want to thank you" She glanced at the ground. Her voice was deep and rich. Water dropped down from her eyes.

He tried to form words, but he and his kind didn't really traffic in them all that often. Instead, he closed the distance between them, and took her in his arms.

What happened next was inevitable. There was nothing flora-like about the human body, so he had no real comparison. She was soft, and the sap beneath her skin was warm. As she touched him, she mistook his firmness for musculature. It was an act born of instinct when he planted the seed in her womb. It was only after she left him in the glen that he realized the gravity of what he had done.

For years, Jack pretended that it hadn't happened. A million things could have transpired. Maybe she lost the baby, or terminated the pregnancy. Maybe he just *thought* he impregnated her. In the years that followed, Jack moved away from the urban landscape, and went deeper into the forest. He spent a couple of years rooted to one place, and left his duties to his brothers and sisters behind. But, in the back of his mind, in his soul, he knew that his child was out there, in the unnatural world. Her true nature would begin to assert itself. And then, there was no telling what would happen. It was guilt that drove him back, and fear for his daughter.

When she got back home, Mom was still in the strange bubble of time, watching Sister Vivian in an infinite loop. She hid her glass tree at the back of a drawer and sat down on the couch.

"Mom," she said. The bubble popped, the spell was ended.

Mom looked at her groggily, as if she'd been awakened from a deep sleep. She was confused. That wild and vulnerable look bought tears to Mabel's eyes. She forgave her mother everything, every boundary she'd set in her way. She understood that, now. Mom was only trying to protect her, not only from her self, but from what ever was out there. Mabel went to her mother, and threw her arms around her. She held her, and for a moment, felt safe. Mom held her back, and stroked her hair.

"Baby," she said.

A forest of glass trees is around her. When the wind blows, the leaves tinkle, and some of them shatter. She moves through the forest barefoot, stepping on translucent shards of leaves. But her foot doesn't bleed, because they are made of glass, too. In fact, the shattered leaves are absorbed into her clear body, and become a part of her. Now she can understand what the

glass trees are singing to her. She doesn't like their song.

Mabel is not alone. She feels her mother beside her. Unlike her, though, she is fully clothed. And there are a thousand hairline cuts on her face. Her blood is bright red—it is cerise—against the green darkness.

"I thought he was Jesus," says Cerise, her mother. "He was beautiful. After all, he'd saved me from those men, and from myself. He had light surrounding him, and his eyes were so kind, so ancient. I just had see if he was real, or if he was just some sick hallucination. I found out that he was real. But he wasn't Jesus at all. He was something evil. He was demon – a monster. And I found I was carrying his child...."

Blood spilled from her wounds like tears. Mom's eyes were dry.

"But, Mom, that means...that I'm..."

"Shh, child. I tried to save you. That's when I found Sister Vivian, before she was on TV. She said that if I prayed hard enough, if I made it right, that we might save you..."

Mabel looks at her nude, glass body. She hears the forest singing in her, and she can't shut it up. Wood and bark and water and sap and roots are all their own language that she understands in some sense. She's the link between tree and soil and air.

"Save me," says Mabel. "Please. I can be good."

Her mother smiles, and though her face is streaked with blood, Mabel feels safe.

Then the forest shatters, shards fly everywhere. The crystals become a part of her body, even as they turn her mother into a ribbon of brown flesh and cerise liquid—

Mabel woke up with a jolt, her heart racing. The room spun around her for a couple of moments before she regained her bearings. She didn't remember her dream. She never did. She'd been having them for a month, after the day that she'd been invisible for a few hours. The vague, shadowy forms of trees left afterimages in her mind. The light from her digital alarm guided her to her bedroom door. After a splash of cold water on her face and a drink from the fridge, she returned to her room, turning on the light. She intended to read the Bible until she got sleepy again. That always did the trick, the words in red and black blurring together. But she noticed a stain on the sheets beneath the upturned covers. It was thick and amber with fragments of something in it. As she moved to the bed, she felt for the first time since waking up moistness in her panties. Examining the stain closely, Mabel saw wood and crumbled leaves floating in the honey liquid. She smelled damp earth and sweet sap rising from her bed, and her body.

The full import of what this meant hit her.

It rose up through her throat and filled her mouth. The vomit that spilled out was sweet and vegetable-tasting. It was brown and clear, like maple syrup. Mabel fainted.

She woke up in a puddle of the strange liquid.

It's not a dream.

The stained covers, the leaves and saps oozing out of her: she balled the sheets up, and cleaned the mess on the floor. In the bathroom, she cleaned herself as silently as she could, not to wake Mom. This was a secret that she could not share. She used one of her Mom's pads, figured out how to use it.

She spent the rest of the night reading random bits of the Bible, flicking through the thin pages, looking for a verse or parable that could save her.

Tree-shaped, life moved by without words. It was wind, air, and soil. It was the rhythm of the earth, the creatures that hid in vines and leaves, the textures and temperatures of existence. But there was always a piece of him that stayed awake, a splinter of consciousness that understood language and logic and purpose.

This tiny piece of humanity stirred now. He heard her, changing and suffering, even though she was miles away. It could not be ignored. It was like a sound, but it wasn't exactly audible. It was a scent that burned, a ray of light that screamed. He wasn't completely healed but Jack knew that there wasn't time. He had to do something for Mabel.

It was the blood—the sap—that connected them, that sang in both his and her veins. It spilled images into her, into him:

A fat woman against an unreal sky.

Prayers to a bearded white man.

Glass trees that writhed against a neon night.

Jack felt her pain as well. The dull ache of menstruation, the gases that she drowned in, ozone, fluorocarbon, perfume. Each step on pavement bought with it the crying of the earth as it was imprisoned in fake stone. Each breath was a knife wound.

He sang to her, in a song of wood, weed and wind. It was a song of summons. It took its rhythm from the growing of things, its melody from wind, its structure from sunlight. He sang it, even as he changed and became man-shaped.

When he was finished, he added his human voice to the song.

"Mabel," he sang. "Daughter..."

It was night when her fever finally broke. There had been days when the difference between waking and sleeping were indistinguishable. Every moment was filled with pain and horrible visions. Faces swam before her, her mother's, Sister Vivian's and others she barely recognized. Their voices and prayers meant nothing to her. What language were they speaking in? Her room spun. She sweated chlorophyll, and peed a strange, thick orange urine. Her stomach rejected food, even water. Mabel's limbs stiffened, stretched and ached for—for something. Light? She craved it, being locked away from the light that spilled just outside.

Through most of it, though, she heard a voice. It was calming, and sent the horrible melting visions to sleep, dampened the cacophony of sounds, and dulled her pain. The sound was soothing and green. It was dark, but promised light.

Mabel sat up, hearing the voice. Her mother was asleep in a chair next to her bed. Her face was crushed in slumber, the mouth slightly open. There was no need to wake her.

In the shower, Mabel came alive again. Water sluiced down her body Her dry skin drank it down. Flakes of dead skin came off her, revealing a new bronzy-brown skin beneath. The flakes went down the drain like leaves. Even her feet, standing in the water, tingled. When she stepped out of the shower, she felt euphoric. Every cell in her body sang, adding a counter melody to the green song that encompassed everything. A glass forest, pierced with sunlight, splashed with prisms appeared in her mind. The green song pulled her.

Her mother was still slumped over on the chair. Mabel placed her in a soundless, lightless bubble of time after she kissed her, and quickly dressed.

Outside, the air was gritty and cool. The streetlights burned. Impurities speckled in front of her, dust, pollen, chemicals. They were like holes in film, staticky scratches and tears that danced before her eyes. As she walked on the sidewalk, she could feel the earth pressed beneath them, the graveyard of aborted seeds and the worms that ate them, Mabel felt nauseous. She leaned against a wall, steadying herself.

Voices babbled in the distance, and looking up, Mabel saw a group of teenaged boys staggering up the block towards her. One of them paused, spotting her. Their conversation became more animated.

Don't let them see me, she thought, and slipped into a bubble where everything was green and prismatic. She saw through facets, and laughed at the boys' confusion. She also felt better. The wave of nausea subsided, and she could no longer feel the ground beneath her feet, and hear the screaming beneath the pavement.

She knew that she was heading towards Dryad Park when she started walking again. That was where the song was coming from, and where the strange man was. She was only a little afraid. Maybe he could explain what was happening to her.

As soon as she set foot in the forest's ground, Mabel felt a bolt of energy suffuse her body. Green and dark and strong. The air in the forest was pure. She opened her lungs and drank it in. The song was audible here. Notes stroked her ears and skin. She shed the green bubble, added it to the tones of the song.

He emerged, clothed in leaves and berries. His dreadlocks were vines, his dark skin had the texture of bark. The moonlight illumined him clearly.

"Mabel," he said. His voice cracked, as if he didn't use it often.

She wasn't surprised that he knew her name. In fact, she was annoyed by it. She stood her ground, ignoring the intricacies of the music that swirled around her—the song of the forest.

"Why did you do this to me?"

"I...I fell in love with your mother. I couldn't help myself." He looked chastened.

"Well. No wonder she didn't—she never told me about you. At least you aren't in jail." She laughed. For some reason, this struck her as absurd.

He looked miserable, his foliage trembling with nervousness.

"You can stop it, can't you? I mean, I don't want to be like you." She knew it was a lie even as she spoke it. She had never felt so alive in her life, the energy of earth and air pulsing through her bones with its wild music.

"I...I don't know," he said.

It was beautiful, beyond anything she had words for. Everything. The ground, the sky, the moonlight. Her blood stirred. She belonged here. The soles of her feet longed to dig in the ground, touch the earth.

I've punished him enough, Mabel thought.

She moved to him, and gave him a hug. Tentatively, he hugged her back.

SAPLING

Jack felt her against him, and the ache he had felt for ages slowly fell away. He felt her skin toughen into bark and her hair soften into moss.

She added her song to his, and to the forest's.

Mauve's Quilt

Mauve

The sky was coming undone. She could see a patch where the fabric had frayed. One of the stars was about to fall, its rhinestone glitter askew. She found that she didn't really care all that much. There was a time when she would have jumped up with her needle, and repaired any imperfection immediately. Now, the tear in space only caused the briefest flicker of concern.

She wasn't bored, exactly. Even now, the sheer beauty of the field where she lay, with its lilacs, irises, and hydrangeas took her breath away. It was just that she was so alone here. And she would always be alone, until the world she made ended. How would it end? With a slow unraveling, as time, moths, and dust dimmed her colors and her life. Her life would end in silence.

She knew it was wrong, what she was feeling. It had the texture of sin.

She stood up, and climbed up into the broken sky.

Quentin

The attic was the color of a secret, a vague and shadowy tone. Quentin searched through in the half-light, picking out patterns. He saw a skeletal hat rack, a broken rocking chair, a shelf full of mangled toys. Bears without eyes and dolls with cracked skulls watched him as he moved through the room, ducking beams. There was a bookcase full of dusty volumes with old style typography .

He found an old hope chest wedged against the far wall. Opening it released a scent of cedar mingled with potpourri and mothballs. It was like opening a coffin. A quilt was folded at the bottom of the chest, nested in dried petals that crumbled as he lifted it out. It was soft and cool to the touch.

His father called his name. He took the sweet-smelling quilt down the ladder with him.

Quentin unfolded the quilt on his bed. A few withered petals drifted to the floor. The quilt was floral, six square panels against a deeply purple background of interlocking violets. The two bottom panels had flowers of different hues of purple: lavender, mauve, and plum. The two panels above had appliquéd moths of grey and silver, one with folded wings praying over the throat of a flower, the other with its wings open. The final two squares showed a sky of dark blue. Most of the sequins that starred the sky had fallen away. He flipped the quilt over, and saw a wild explosion of bright purple blossoms. Their cups were black as eyes, and stared at him.

Where did you get that ugly thing? That's what Mom would have said. She'd hated crafty things. This was too afghan-like for her taste.

"Hey." Quentin turned, saw Dad in the doorway. He was disheveled and sweating. One of his fingers had a cut on it that was still bleeding. Dad was a mess; Mom would have had a band-aid on it, at the very least.

"Hey."

"What did you find in the attic?" Dad stepped into the room, then stepped back, as if he wasn't sure if he was invited in.

Quentin turned back to the quilt. "Nothing. Just a bunch of junk."

Dad lingered in the doorway for a couple of uncomfortable seconds. "Well," he said finally, "When you're finished, maybe you can help me in the kitchen?"

The heat wrapped itself around Quentin like a wet towel in spite of the air-conditioning. There was a fan in his room set to full blast, and he was naked beneath a single sheet, on top of the quilt.

What I am doing here? Summer in Chicago wasn't as brutal as it was here. Everything here sucked. There was nothing to do, everything was at least 40 minutes away by car, and even the people moved slowly, as if they were drugged. *Dad is crazy.* Quentin knew that. Mom was the one who held them both together. In his own way, Dad was as lost as Quentin himself was.

The quilt is cool.

It was true. On a whim, Quentin went underneath the covers. Miraculously, it was cooler underneath the covers than it was above. His face was warmer than the part of his body that was submerged beneath. He dipped his head under.

He fell into a fractal. He felt the fur of African violets brush his body. The world kept getting bigger and bigger, until the pixels were the size of windows. He ended up straddling a thread the size of a suspension bridge that hung over endless, frozen folds of water that was bright purple. Gauze fell over his face, enfolded him, and tickled his face like spider webs. Through the tinted mesh, he saw his room. Except that it was different. Next to a canopy bed, a black woman sat in a rocking chair. An unfinished quilt was folded on her lap. She was working on it intently.

It grew slowly beneath her fingers. Her skin was dark, the color of coffee, and her short hair was styled in some old-fashioned way that he'd seen in black and white movies. She wore a black dress with purple flowers on it. He watched her for a long time, placing pieces of fabric together and cutting thread with scissors. A silver needle pierced fabric.

When he woke up, African violets stained the air around him with their color.

Mauve

"Come on, baby, it will be alright." Momma held her hand. She gave it a squeeze. Mauve smiled in response.

"OK," she said.

The path to the house wasn't so long after all. It was just a little overgrown. The two-story house did have a certain masculine charm about it. Two saplings with infant magnolias grew in the yard, and there were flowering bushes, forsythia and, of course, azaleas. Beds of phlox hemmed in these bushes. The house still had a decrepit feel to it. But the cold feeling in the pit of her stomach would change with time, wouldn't it? The lack of color made Mauve feel queasy. But she didn't want to upset her mother; she'd worked so long and hard for the two of them. And now, she was getting sicker. Her joints ached with arthritis, and she had a touch of gout. This *had* to work out.

"It's not so scary,"

"That's right, baby," said Momma, "You'll do fine here. I know you will."

They walked up the stairs and onto the wide porch. It was cool and shaded there. Mauve shivered, in spite of herself. She wished she'd worn her shawl. Momma rang the doorbell. A deep sound echoed through the depth of the house. Professor Foxworth opened the door. He was tall, thin, and pale, like a birch tree. His bald head was egg shaped and fringed with wispy white hair. Bushy tufts of sideburns framed his bespectacled face and his eyes were a watery shade of blue. His eyes were so washed out they were almost colorless.

"Hello, Doreen. You must be Mauve." Mauve saw that he didn't look at either her or her mother. She took his hand, which was limp and cool. It was a disinterested grip. He didn't smile.

Both women followed the professor into the house. The ceilings were high, the woodwork ornate. Mauve felt as if she were being swallowed by some beast. The professor's thin shadow on the wall was skeletal. The women were lead to a study outfitted with a large desk. Thousands of books lined the shelves; the spines were in dull, uninteresting colors. The professor sat in a high-backed chair behind the desk. Mauve noticed that her mother didn't sit down on the green velvet couch that faced the desk. The professor didn't seem to notice this, and did not give any permission. *The couch looks uncomfortable anyway.* Mauve looked around the dark room while her mother and the professor spoke.

"I can't offer your daughter much in the way of compensation,

Doreen. But, she will have her own room, and, and use of the kitchen."

"You are too kind." Momma looked down at her feet. Mauve followed her gaze, and became hypnotized by the faded pattern in the rug. There was a repeating circular arrangement of birds and vines. If you stared long enough, the amber birds moved slightly.

"...can cook a few dishes well. Nothing too complicated, sir," Momma was saying.

"I hardly expect gourmet fare. I am sure what she can provide will be sufficient."

"Sir, I was wondering, though...In addition to Sunday, could she have Saturday evening off as well? So she could spend the night? That way, I would have more time with her..."

The professor paused. "I see no reason why not. Though, occasionally, I do entertain on Saturday evenings. In which case, I would be in need of her help."

"Of course, of course, sir."

"Yes, well. Mauve, do you have any questions about your duties?"

She looked up from the birds and vines. Both the professor and her mother were looking at her expectantly.

"I would like to see the room where I'll be sleeping-if that is OK."

He stood up from the desk, all his long limbs straightening themselves out with audible cracks. "Please follow me."

They walked up a staircase and down a hall full of sepia photographs of severe-faced men and women. They all frowned at Mauve. She felt out of place, in her purple dress. It was too bright; the house wanted to devour her, with its browns, greys, and blacks. The professor opened a door at the end of the hall. The room was bare, painted an off-white color, with a twin bed and single dresser. The floor had no rugs. Sunlight illuminated the room, at an oblique angle. At once, she saw the walls painted pale purple, a rug in the same shade. She could buy new curtains. This would never be like at her room at home, but she could try her best to bring something of home to this cold place.

"It's not much," the professor said, "but it should be sufficient. You may, of course, decorate the room anyway you see fit."

"Can I paint it, sir?" she said before she thought of it.

Momma touched her shoulder, signaling her disapproval.

The white-haired man paused thoughtfully-still not looking at the women. "I don't see why not."

Her purple dress burned in the room, an iris in a sea of white and pale yellow.

The professor left the room. "A quick tour of the house is in order, don't you agree, Doreen?"

"Yes sir," Momma answered, following him.

Mauve gave one last look at the pale room before leaving.

Quentin

Life in Azalea limped along, crippled by the ever-present heat. Quentin tried to make the best of it, biking through sedate neighborhoods filled with old mansions and seemingly older residents. He felt out of place here. But then, he felt out of place everywhere. Blue-haired ladies with huge hats waved at him as he glided by. He biked to another section of town, and saw diners and boutique shops; they were never crowded. Further on, he saw neighborhoods full of more recent housing, with dull beige aluminum siding and matchbox-sized yards. The people that stood outside of these places were mostly darker, black and Hispanic. The twenty-first century was in evidence here; he heard rap music booming from car speakers. The neighborhood where he lived was trapped in a snow globe. It was the 1950s, stagnant and fossilized. Quentin felt odd whenever he switched on his computer. It was sleek and modern, white and liquid crystal. It was out of place.

The doorbell was so seldom used, that Quentin didn't know what the sound was. He put the computer to sleep. A screensaver of floating African violets spun on a darkened screen. He moved through the house quickly, expertly avoiding the points were the floor creaked.

He opened the door, and saw a large black woman in pale green suit. Her fat legs were encased in white stockings. She carried a bakery box in front of her.

"Welcome to the neighborhood," she said. She held out the box to him. "I'm Eula Banks. I live at the end of the block, in the yellow Tudor on the corner. Are your parents home?"

It took Quentin a moment to remember how to speak. "No," he said as he took the box, "Dad's at work. Mom's-I don't have a mother. I mean, she's passed."

Eula Banks' face fell. "I'm sorry to hear that."

"It's OK."

"Was it recent?"

"Yes. I mean, in March."

The silence after that lasted forever. He couldn't take the look she gave him. He saw Mom, pale and hairless, blue veins like trees underneath her waxen skin. He saw the shadows on her coffin, purple-black, like the shadows in the attic above.

He said, "What's in the box?"

"My lemon chess pie." She stepped into the foyer, and looked around. *Quentin, where are you manners?* He heard Mom's voice in his head.

"Come on in," he said. "I think there's leftover coffee."

Eula said, while sipping microwaved coffee, "There was a girl who worked there, a girl I knew from church. Mauve Willoughby. After her mother died, we'd take turns visiting her. She had no-one, you know, no husband or brothers or sisters. Plus, she was a little slow, if you know what I mean.

"She took over her mother's job, as a housekeeper for the professor who lived here. She was a sweet girl. I remember going up to her room in that house, one time. I was maybe thirteen or so. Her room was the brightest one in the house, full of flowers and bold colors. All purples and magentas.

"One day, she didn't come to church, and no one saw her again. Her employer, the professor, only told the police that she was missing when he'd been annoyed by the church folk.

"Most people thought she'd run away, though to where, who knows? Some us think that she might have, you know, died by her own hand somewhere..."

Eula's voice trailed off. Quentin knew that she saw Mauve in the distance, in her flowers and fabrics. She shook her head.

Mauve

The quilt was growing in her hands, stitch by stitch. Flowers and moths of purple bloomed and flew against a white background. Mauve became the silver needle, piercing the skin of quilt, tattooing it with images. Soft music from the radio played in the background. The light from the lamp next to her bed guided her patient movements. Moments like these, she could forget the last few months.

The feel of a satin petal reminded her of the satin lining the coffin where her mother lay. They had filled in the cracks of her face with powder, hiding age marks. Momma wore bright red lipstick, something she would have never done in life. Smudged red circles were painted over her sunken cheeks. She had been laid out against the pristine white satin, surrounded by flower bouquets and flickering candles. She still looked out of place: a shriveled up dead thing, no different from the day when Mauve had found her sitting on the living room.

In went the needle, joining fabric together with a thin thread.

The Professor had given her a week off, to attend to the funeral and her mother's estate. He hadn't come to the funeral, even though his mother had worked for him for over ten years. His absence was glaring, but not unwelcome. He was a strange, distant man, she found in the months she lived with him. It was a week of planning, of numbers and papers and signatures. It was a week of days that wouldn't end, and of tons of food that was untouched. It was a week of people from the church giving her sad looks, strangers stroking her shoulders, prayers, and sleepless nights. Honestly, it was somewhat a relief to get back to work. Then she didn't have to think about it. There was just a silent house of dust devils and ancient furniture. A house her mother cleaned for ten years. There, in a patch of sunlight, beneath the magnolia tree, in the pupils of the Professor's distracted eyes, she could see Momma.

Out went the needle, emerging with an umbilical cord trailing behind.

It had been three months since then. Church ladies still visited her, coming to the back of the house, laden with cakes, pies and other treats. Poor Mauve, their eyes said. Each bite of the treats whispered, It's so sad. Each reassuring pat on her back spoke, You know she's a little slow, but Doreen looked out for her.

Mauve snapped the thread between her teeth.

Quentin

Quentin dreamed of African violets. Their heavy cups swayed in the breeze, their open throats tasting the air. They grew out of an earth rich and smooth as skin, and reached for a sky that was cobalt and black at the same time. When he woke from these dreams, images burned on the air. It was like the light itself was bleeding. He woke up, surrounded by a field of wild flowers on fire. The woman was always there. She never seemed to notice him. She was so involved with her sewing, and what she made was so beautiful and intricate that he didn't feel slighted in the least.

She was child sized, with a gentle swelling bosom and curving hips. Her face was kind of gaunt, her cheeks sunken, as if she had lost her natural plumpness during a long illness. Her dark brown eyes, the color of maple syrup, were sad and downcast. But she smiled as she worked, making petals, earth and sky.

He wanted to touch her. It felt odd. He didn't like touching people. He twitched involuntarily whenever his mother had touched him, or his father patted his back. His space was his own; he didn't like it to be invaded. But he wanted to touch her, to feel her skin, and blood pulsing in her veins. He could take her sadness away, maybe.

Once, she looked up and saw him. She was far away, in a wrinkle of hill. He waved at her.

Mauve

Mauve laid down the batting for her quilt. It was mounds of white cotton. She felt it with her hands, running them over the clouds. But this batch wasn't soft enough. It didn't float. It wasn't buoyant. She wanted a quilt so soft and light that it would send her to the place in her dreams, the hills where there were millions of wild flowers that swayed in the breeze. Surely, it was heaven. The swirl of lavender and green, the sky of robin's egg blue was a place where God lived. Over one of the hills, her mother would come striding, with swan wings sprouting from her Sunday best dress of black and blue fabric. Mauve had visited the sanctuary of silk flowers last night. She knew that it was dream. But it wasn't a normal dream. This was a Vision, one like Sister Vivian had in church, when God touched her soul and she spoke in the divine tongue of angels. The Vision was a glimpse, a promise of a golden future in the afterlife. During the dream, she saw an angel in the distance, on one of the hills. His skin had been as pale as cream, his hair white gold. She had smiled at him warmly. Was he her Guardian?

"Mauve."

The professor's voice broke into her reverie. She put the clouds back into their bag, and went to attend to him.

In his study, a pipe smoldered, next to scatted sheets of yellow legal paper marked with his cryptic scrawl.

"Yes, sir."

She curtsied.

He didn't look up.

Wreathed in smoke, like a Hollywood gangster, he gave his instruction: "A cup of Earl Grey tea, and some crackers."

In the kitchen, Mauve set the kettle to boil, rummaged through the shelf where the tea was kept. She found three canisters. Two of them had the letter E on them. It took a short while for the sequence of letters to reveal their meaning to her. Mauve thought that letters where magic. They changed their places and shifted their shapes before her eyes. This didn't happen to other people; she understood that. She found it sad that others couldn't see the hidden movement of things.

When she set the tea and crackers down on the professor's desk, he didn't acknowledge her. She noticed that a few books written by him were on the table. *A Study of the Feeble-Minded*, one of the titles read.

"Mauve?" He looked up at her, his spectacle lenses flashing with late afternoon light. "Was there something else?"

She realized that she'd been staring at the book for a while, and she must have slipped into one of her "states," as her mother called them.

"No, sir," she said, curtsied, and left the room.

She worked on her quilt that evening, slowly shifting through fabrics with her favorite color. She cut the fabric into isosceles triangles that evening, listening to the radio, until she dozed off.

She woke a while later, disturbed by the crick in her neck. The lamp on her nightstand was still on, and she'd dropped her scissors. As she stretched her neck to the left, she saw that the door to her room was slightly ajar. She saw a shadow rushing away.

Mauve jumped. She listened for footsteps, and checked the hallway as she closed the door. He was long gone.

Quentin

Quentin is wrapped in a cocoon of purple fibers.

The field where she works blooms before his eyes, hill after hill of lavender, salmon, and mauve, spreading out as far as the eye can see. She floats in the air, stitching glittering, jewel-encrusted fabric to the cobalt drape of the sky. Her needle flashes. The star shapes flame and glow after she's placed them. Her feet hover over blossom heads.

Hill after hill passes, a blur of green, farmhouses and cows. Dad is trying to talk to him.

"I'm guessing that you're pretty mad at me. I don't blame you. It must seem like I'm crazy. I've uprooted you from the only life that you know, away from your friends, just when you might need familiar things the most...."

Heat mirages dance on the horizon, and static from the radio bleeds songs in shards. The world is full of ghosts, ghosts of sound, ghosts of the road.

"...I had to get away, Quentin. Chicago was full of her. She was everywhere. And when this job offer came, I...."

Quentin sees plowed fields, as neat as squares on a quilt. They pass an ostrich farm. The tall, skinny birds look out of place in this world.

"It's not so bad, you know. I grew up here. Small town life has its own pace, and it's much more relaxing..."

They pass by a field of flowers. Miles upon miles of purple blossoms spill out over the edge of the world. They nod their heads in the breeze from the passing traffic.

"It's OK," Quentin says, to shut his dad up.

Mauve

Afterwards, things went back to normal. She cooked his meals, cleaned the house, and went to church on Sundays. Her days and weeks were routine, and they slipped into months and seasons. Sunny mornings and grey rain-filled ones were the same to her. The day was divided into tasks and chores, and the nights were filled with dreamless slumber.

The times she had to speak to the professor weren't difficult at all. She could look straight at him, and not see his face, or his body. He was an indistinct shape, an Absence given form. He was nothing. She didn't hear his voice. The instructions he gave just appeared in her mind somehow. She didn't examine why too closely.

She would take her dinner in her room, but she wouldn't eat much. Food made her nauseous. At first, she thought that maybe something lived inside her belly. But it was clear that nothing lived there after a while. She still bled. She didn't eat, because food was connected to living.

Her evenings were special, the time of day she always looked forward to. There was a ritual to it all. First, Mauve lit a few candles, mostly for effect. She would turn on the radio, and then work on the quilt. As the silver needle sparkled through the fabric, she would go to the place where flowers covered the hillside, and the stars spangled the sky. She sewed herself inside the world of thread, stitch and fabric. The pattern of the quilt became clear then, in this space. She made an endless field of flowers, a world where angels watched her and love was just over the horizon. It was a small bit of time, as small as thimble, but it was hers. Petals were bright here, and they never withered.

Once, she caught him looking at her. This was before he became the Absence.

It was a terrifying moment, because she truly thought it couldn't happen again. She'd bitten his finger, and peed on him. But, she recalled, that hadn't stopped him.

She'd thrown the unfinished quilt over her body. It was a childish thing to do, the sort of thing a feeble-minded fool might do. Of course, he would rip the quilt off her body, and rip her clothes, like he did before. And he would burn her insides.

Beneath the quilt was cool. And she dove into it, the sea of flowers. Cool iris and furry African violet, hydrangea, and blue bell. Tulips covered her face. The flowers grew out of her brown earth body, and hid her female form. The professor blinked, not seeing her, and moved on.

Now, he could never see her properly, just as she could never see him. She was earth and fabric. Both her earth body and her real body were protected by flowers.

Quentin

"I'm going to catch a movie, Quentin. Why don't you come with me?"

"No, I'm OK." Quentin stared at the computer screen, and watched the slow dance of equalization bars. Soundwaves were like thread, he thought. Strands that could be stretched across a loom, and turned into a tapestry...

"Son?" His father still stood in the doorway. "You sure? I mean, we don't have to go to a movie. We can eat out. I heard that there's a great place about 20 minutes away that makes excellent Italian food. It's been there forever."

Quentin glanced at his father. He saw nothing. His face, the arrangement of his features, was a mystery to him. Was he sad? Was Quentin supposed to react, somehow?

He tried, "Maybe some other time."

Even when he is awake, Quentin sees Mauve everywhere, both the color and the woman. It's there, on a woman's scarf. He sees it in the hair dye of a young punk woman, or on the roof of a gazebo covered in bougainvillea. She would like that, he thinks.

Quentin waits for the night, when he can curl up beneath Mauve's quilt. He doesn't always see her quiet, woven world. But she's always there. Satiny-soft, he sometimes feels her swimming within the quilt. Something brushes him, in the thin mesh between them.

Quentin saw her in the field of purple flowers. He was closer to her than ever before. He watched for a while, as she repaired the wing of a moth. The creature patiently hovered over a tulip as Mauve's needle healed the wing. She worked with such precision and concentration, she hardly noticed when he walked up behind her. When she finished, the silver moth fluttered away.

"Mauve," he said to her softly.

She faced him. Mauve was shorter than he was, and her eyes were a lovely shade of clear brown, between honey and amber. Her dress of violets moved with the breeze, with the rest of the flowers of the field that she'd made. She held the needle in front of her like a knife.

"I didn't make you," she said, after a while. "I didn't think anyone could find me, ever. How did you find me?"

Quentin shrugged. "How did you make this?" His gesture took in the woven world.

She lowered the needle-knife, perhaps conceding the point. They both sat down on the soft earth, and watched the unchanging sky above them.

"It's coming apart, you know," she said.

Quentin saw a section of the sky that was threadbare. In the distance, a few hills had faded. A few stars dangled, threatening to fall.

"I guess you can't stay here forever." He glanced at her. Mauve stared out into space, maybe remembering why she'd come here in the first place. "He's gone. Long gone."

When she turned back to him, there were tears in her eyes. Her eyes glistened like stars. She wiped them away, and stood up, and picked up a frayed violet. Mauve tore off a damaged petal, and let it fall to ground.

Quentin woke up covered in dried petals. He sat up, and found that the quilt was destroyed, in pieces around the room. Petals, bright and withered, filled his bed and spilled out on the floor. Some were soft as new skin while others were blackened and curled. A few dead moths were strewn about, their wings full of holes, their filigree bodies forever frozen.

"Mauve!" The word escaped his lips. In the corner of the room, he saw an unmolested swath of fabric on the floor. It was the fallen sky, pierced with stars. As he moved towards it, his barefoot stepped on a still cooling chip of heaven. It burned him, so he jumped back, landing on his rear.

The piece of sky moved. There was something underneath it. Or within it, struggling to get out.

Time unknotted and unraveled, as the fragment rose above the floor. It floated, becoming an upside down V, the skirt of a dress. Mauve formed out of fabric. A torso, two arms burst through thread and ether.

Mauve stood in a puddle of thread, dead petals and moths, wearing a dress of purple flowers that glowed. She looked at Quentin. He couldn't really say what emotion played across her face, but he knew that it wasn't fear.

"Welcome back, Mauve," he said, because it sounded like the right thing to say.

Lyes

Sheri always felt that images spoke to her. Just not *literally*.

She was doing her thesis on the images of African Americans in advertising. *The Semiotics of Subjugation: African American Images Filtered Through the Hegemonic Veil* was the title of her project. Her bedroom/office was littered with ads from magazines, various vintage products, and posters.

She was poring over a recent printout of her manuscript, vigorously marking it, when she heard someone say, "You shore do look hungry."

Sheri glanced up from her densely embedded text. She looked at the radio and the television. Both were off. She shook her head. 'Must be getting tired,' she thought. She briefly considered going out for coffee. It would be too much trouble, and she'd lose her momentum, she decided, and went back to editing.

"Poor honey chile, you look like you needs a good nap."

There was no mistaking it this time.

Sheri looked up to find a white apron in front of her face. As her eyes moved upwards they took in a large woman in a flame-red hoop skirt, a checkered blouse with a bright bandana on her head. She had a warm face with a nice smile. She smelled of maple syrup. It was Auntie Clabber, circa 1930. She fell back onto her bed.

"Ah, shucks, honey chile. Ain't no reason to be afraid. I jes saw that you looked mighty hungry. And you shore could use a stack o' flapjacks—"

Sheri rolled off her bed, scattering the pages. "Who— What are you doing in my bedroom?"

Auntie Clabber threw her head back and laughed: "Chile, you look like you jes saw a hain't!"

But she *had*. She saw a poster against a wall, and noticed that it was blank. Apparently, Auntie Clabber had somehow *stepped* out of her poster. Which, of course, was ridiculous. Sheri left the large woman in her bedroom.

Closing the bathroom door behind her, Sheri headed for the sink. She turned the faucet on, and splashed cold water onto her face. *I definitely need a cup of coffee; I've been working too hard.* Maybe she would go out to a café or a Starbucks. A nice, dark cup of espresso with a wedge of lemon should clear the fog from her mind. She couldn't afford to sleep; her first draft was due in two days.

After toweling herself off, Sheri went back to her bedroom. Auntie Clabber was still there, but she wasn't alone. She was in conversation with another woman. This other woman was tall, statuesque, and the color of café au lait. She wore a powder blue dress and her hair was styled in a Marcel wave. She was perfumed. Lavender, probably. Sheri recognized her as the model for Miss Lula's Lightening Cream.

Auntie Clabber was saying to Lula, "You shore do make it sound mighty in-ter-estin'. I think I'll try me some."

"Thank you, darling. Let me know if you have any questions." Lula's voice was soft and glamorous. She handed the older woman a small container of the cream.

Both women turned towards Sheri simultaneously.

"Hello, darling," said Lula. She smiled at her. There was something reptilian about that smile. She glided over to where Sheri was, like Morticia Addams. "Care to try some lightening cream? It goes on smoothly. It feels like silk. It doesn't burn, like those other creams—"

Sheri moved back, shrinking into the door frame.

"Honey chile, is you still scared?"

Sheri said, "How the hell did you get here?"

Both ladies were taken aback.

Lula said, in dulcet tones, "Such rough language is hard on my ears, darling."

Auntie Clabber tsked, "She been around sailors an' other Godless folkes."

"I—I—" sputtered Sheri. "Get out of my house."

They ignored this.

Instead, Lula opened a jar of lightening cream. She waved the pale mixture, which looked like whipped egg whites, under Sheri's nose. Lavender drifted up.

"Get that thing out of my face!"

"Oh, darling, I just know you'd love it. You could be the color of caramel, or amber. You'd look simply *divine*—"

"I don't need—put that thing *down*. I don't need to look like candy or tree sap. I look fine. Now, just what the hell are you doing in my apartment? How did you get in here?"

Again, they both ignored her. They were too busy laughing. The lady in blue shivered and tittered. The lady in red shuddered and rumbled.

"What's so damn funny?

"Darling, your language—"

"I was jes laughin' cause you say you don't need lightening cream. Honey chile, you cute as a button, but you black as 'lasses."

Sheri was no longer shrinking against the wall. She was too angry to be afraid. She said, "I *look* just fine. 'The darker the berry, the sweeter the juice,' I always say."

Auntie Clabber laughed again, "If that's so, honey, you could give a man diabetes!"

Lula and Auntie Clabber exploded with laughter.

Sheri walked by them to the telephone. She was about to dial 911, and tell the police that there were a couple of escaped lunatics in her apartment, when she *sensed* another presence. The smell of lye heralded its arrival. Sheri turned to face a woman rising from an old magazine ad. At first the figure was black, white and yellow. Sheri watched with fascination and horror as the woman was born from the magazine pages. When she was full-sized, she changed to a more natural color. She wore a flowing white gown and her hair was a stiff, artificial waterfall. Her brown skin glistened; it was iridescent. There she was in the flesh, Beulah, the Lye Queen.

"Evenin', ladies," said Beulah.

"How you doin'?" added Auntie Clabber.

"What a pleasure to see you, darling."

"I overheard you talking to the ladies," Beulah began. Her voice was bright, but had an oily undertone. "As long as you're gonna lighten your skin, you might as well straighten your hair."

Beulah produced a can of her relaxer, and opened it. At once, Sheri was enveloped in an overwhelming miasma of lye. It tickled and burned her nose.

"I don't need my hair straightened."

"Oh, *please*," said the lady in white, annoyed.

"Darling, how do you ever expect to get a man?" said the lady in blue.

"Honey chile," said the lady in red, "you look like a bush woman. All you needs is to be nekked."

The three figures began advancing on her. They flashed their emblems at her. Lye, pale cream, and a stack of pancakes drizzled with syrup. They walked slowly, like old movie vampires.

"I don't need my skin lightened, and I hate pancakes!" This last statement was a lie. Sheri didn't care. "Now get out!"

The three women shrugged and moved towards their respective ads. Silently, they melted back into them. They left lingering scents in the air: lavender and lye.

Darshanna always had her head on right. She could clear the cobwebs away.

"Girl, you look like you seen a ghost." Darshanna stood by a bubbling pot of thirteen-bean soup. Sheri's mouth watered, at the thought of the beans soaked in chicken broth, seasoned with curry powder and brown sugar. Darshanna began to crumble sage sausage into the large pot.

"Well, I practically did see a ghost." Sheri was unsure of how to proceed. She took the safer route. "I had a kind of waking dream..."

Darshanna stopped crumbling the sausage and looked at her. Her dreads fanned out like the fronds of a spider fern. There was open curiosity on her face.

Sheri answered her look: "I mean, I was working on the first draft of my thesis, you know, editing it. A hard copy. I can't do it on the computer. I was editing it, when, I saw... Well, I mean, I've worked with these advertisements for so long that I've come to know them. You know what I mean?" Sheri trailed off, losing her nerve.

Darshanna cocked an eyebrow at her. She was as imposing as an Amazon: nearly six feet tall, in a burnished brown-gold pantsuit interrupted with a blouse of royal purple. She wore a necklace of cowry shells, with dangling gazelle earrings.

"I have no idea what you're talking about, girl. Not unless you mean you saw Auntie Clabber tramping around your apartment." Darshanna laughed, a rich, earthy sound, as she turned back to the soup. "Now, why don't you tell me what happened. Start from the beginning."

"Well..." Sheri squeaked. She suddenly felt very small.

Darshanna stopped fussing with the soup. Her shoulders were stiff. She turned around slowly. "What you talkin' about, Willis?"

"I saw Auntie Clabber and Lula the lightening cream woman, and Beulah the Lye Queen. They wanted to straighten my hair, and lighten my skin and make me eat pancakes." Sheri rushed this all out. She was afraid if she didn't barrel through, she would be too embarrassed to finish.

Darshanna laughed, her hair-fronds quivering in time. "Honey, honey, you've been working too hard."

She stepped away from the pot, and enveloped Sheri with a hug. Sheri smelled her sweet, *human* smell.

"You mean, it wasn't real?"

Darshanna released her: "I'm pretty sure, Agent Mulder."

Sheri giggled. "It's just that, it was so strange and kinda spooky. I mean, I had to yell at them, to make them leave me alone. And even then..."

"Shhh. It was just a dream. Now have some soup. It's ready."

Darshanna ladled the soup into a pale orange bowl. She placed the bowl on a plate with a hunk of her custardy cornbread. For a good five minutes, Sheri lost herself in eating the fragrant food. The scents of meat and spices wafted up. There was a sweet note underneath the heat of spice. Sheri would alternate bites of the soup with pieces of the soft, cake-like bread. The cornbread, true to its name, was crowned with soft custard of buttermilk. It melted in her mouth. Sheri only realized now just how tired she'd been. She hadn't tried to go back to sleep after the incident. She'd just stared at the lifeless pages where the phantoms bloomed.

Darshanna broke the silence: "Honey, you should talk to your committee. If you explain to them how much stress you've been under, I'm sure that they'll let up."

Sheri stopped chewing: "No. I'm so close. I've been in school for for-fucking-ever. I'm sick of it. I just wanna get it over with."

Darshanna was silent for a moment. "Sheri, I think that you seeing Uncle Ben hopping around was a message to you. You'd best not ignore it."

Sheri nodded. "'Shanna, I'm not gonna kill myself. I promise you that. It's just that, you know..."

"I know. You want it over with. I hear you, girl. You just don't wanna burn yourself out." Good old Darshanna. She was a warrior, and reality was her battlefield. The things she'd seen were just figments of her imagination. She felt safe; Darshanna's confidence was a cloak that covered them both.

"Thanks, Mom." She finished her soup. "Girl, you gotta give me the recipe for this."

Darshanna shook her head. "No, girl. My grandmom'd kill me."

"I wouldn't tell nobody. I promise."

"Can't. But I can give you a tip."

Sheri leaned forward. Darshanna had gotten up, and was dishing out ice cream for desert.

"Just a drop of it makes all the difference in the world."

"A drop of what?"

Darshanna placed a bowl of white ice cream, sprinkled with raspberries, in front of her. "A drop of maple syrup. Makes it sweet, but it adds a little bit of something that you can't quite put your finger on."

"Thanks, girl. I'll keep that in mind. You'd make Auntie Clabber proud."

Darshanna laughed.

Sheri woke up to a strange smell, tickling her nose. It was naggingly familiar. She couldn't quite put her finger on it. She opened her eyes to the half-light, glancing at the digital clock's green numbers. 6:48AM. Not even full daylight yet. She closed her eyes, ready for at least another hour of sleep. But—she caught just the slightest hint of a whisper. Shadows whisked away in the corner of not-yet closed eyes.

Sheri sat up, frightened. She quickly scanned her bedroom. All was silent, and still. Except—the door to her room was slightly ajar. She distinctly remembered closing it last night. But it was possible...

"Goddammit," she said aloud. She was up; there was really no point in going back to sleep now. Sheri stepped out of the bed, and went to the window. The light of newly risen sun filtered through the chemical wash of smog. A few cars trundled down La Brea Avenue, forerunners of the inevitable traffic jam that occurred daily at 7:00. She heard the kids screaming in the apartment above her as they were getting ready for school. A cool breeze drifted through the screen, tickling the Earth, Wind & Fire T-shirt she wore. The smog today must've been thick; Sheri could *smell* it. There was a singed smell to it.

Sheri went to her bathroom, feeling light-headed. She turned on the bathroom light and looked in the mirror, more out of habit than anything else.

A stranger looked back at her.

Sheri fell back against the door, slamming it shut. After the golden minnows of sleep were blinked away, she approached her image. Of course it was her—under a ton of make-up. Her lips were rouged, a deep ruby color, outlined in black. They were red and swollen, as if she'd just bitten into some luscious tropical fruit and been stained with its juice. The darkness of her skin was hidden beneath a thick layer of some golden-brown powder. Sheri felt her face. It was not powder; it was some kind of paste. She flaked it away, and it fell in cakey scales. The ghost of blush (red fading to pink) was lightly applied to the canvas of her cheeks. Her eyes were centered in twin fans of peacock-green shadow. The perfection of their symmetry frightened and amazed her. And her hair had been slicked back. It was silky and tinted a caramel color. There was even a curl plastered to the center of her forehead, like an obscure musical notation.

"Jesus Christ!" Sheri examined her face, trying to find herself. She was hypnotized by this new mask. *I fucking look like Josephine Baker.*

Sheri recognized the smell at once. She'd mistaken it for the stench of an L.A. morning, but it was worse. It was singed hair smell of relaxers.

What did this all mean? Sheri closed her eyes. She felt the room begin to spin; the golden minnows wriggled free from medicine cabinet, from behind the toilet, beneath the shaggy white bathroom mat. It meant that Darshanna was wrong—that the things she'd seen a couple of days ago were real. They were alive, and come to drive into madness, and make her into their little dress up doll. Sheri giggled nervously. Maybe Darshanna was right: she was simply insane. *Last night, before I went to bed, I put on this makeup, perfectly, not smudging a bit...* Somehow, this was impossible to believe. Sheri knew she was way too clumsy. No, it was easier (if no less disturbing) to believe that these phantom-women had somehow visited her, and given her a makeover.

It put whole new perspective on the term "glamour."

Sheri giggled nervously again. There was really nothing she could do at the moment. They could appear at any time.

She turned on the faucet, and wet a washcloth. Steam wafted up from the curled, thick nap of it.

"I'm taking this shit off," she said. She wasn't sure if anyone heard her. She didn't particularly care.

Sheri finished showering. Under the hot jetting water, she saw that both her toe-and-fingernails had been painted a nice metallic green color. She considered going over to her neighbor Alice's to borrow some remover. But she decided she liked it.

When Sheri walked into the kitchen, she felt like herself. A little unsettled, but otherwise OK. She walked towards the fridge, getting out milk. She noticed that the oven was on. The light was on, shining on something.

She didn't remember making anything to eat last night. The knob was turned up to 200 degrees—barely warm.

Something like relief flooded through her when she opened the oven door and found a warm stack of griddle cakes on a blue Fiesta-ware dish.

Sheri heard muffled voices behind Professor Laetitia Bouchier's door. It was too late to back out now. Still, she cursed Darshanna—Prof. Bouchier (or "La Bouche," as she was informally called) was notoriously temperamental. She didn't suffer excuses; she announced that at the beginning of her classes and seminars. She'd been known to flunk out students at the Eleventh Hour. It was already a legend, how she'd been stalked and harassed by a former failed student of hers. He was now in jail.

Maybe if I act just crazy enough... The thought trailed off. The door to the professor's office opened. A student stood haloed in the palm-latticed sunlight streaming from the office window. The student's face was downcast, and—unmistakably—tears streaked her face. She started to walk down the hallway of the Communication building, mimicking the first steps of the trek of a sorrowful saint. *Excommunication student,* thought Sheri. Her stomach twinged.

"Ms. Alexander, do come in." La Bouche's cigarette-stained contralto beckoned her into her sunlit lair.

Sheri meekly walked into the office, closing the door behind her. Prof. Bouchier was in her customary leather and silk ensemble: black leather pants and boots, pink silk blouse. Her short Afro was shockingly white, in contrast with her dark skin. She was surprisingly wrinkle free for a woman of 64. She was leaning in her armchair, fingering her Shona walking staff, which was as black as the leather she wore. A hand-rolled cigarette rested on a Depression glass candy dish full of butts. It pointed at Sheri accusatorily.

"I was hoping you'd come in," started La Bouche.

"You were?" asked Sheri. Had Darshanna already spoken to her? If she had... Sheri made a mental note to herself to kick Darshanna's ass.

"Yes. Quite frankly, Ms. Alexander, your thesis is D.O.A.. I think it could be better. You are capable of so much more."

Sheri relaxed. "I was feeling the same thing. I had met an impasse, and my writing felt stillborn—"

"Stop brown-nosing, young lady!" La Bouche sat up in her chair and rapped the floor three times with her walking staff. "Flattery will not make me pass your thesis."

Sheri sat back in her chair quickly, as if she'd been singed.

La Bouche continued: "Your writing is dry, inert. It smacks of slavish mimicry. You need to inject life into it. What shows is *understanding* of the terms and materials. But you do not display *mastery*. And you have not yet fallen in love with your subject matter. It has not yet possessed you."

Sheri nodded.

"You need to make these icons of African oppression live and speak."

If she only knew, thought Sheri.

"Two weeks, Ms. Alexander. I give you two weeks more to perform the proper sorcery to enliven your text. That is all. I will inform the rest of the committee."

As Sheri walked out of the Communications building, she felt zapped of strength. She never knew how similar relief and terror felt.

The Dharma Lounge stank, as Sheri knew it would. Old beer, urine and the sweaty miasma of hot perfume stung her nose as she entered into the throng. She could feel it creeping on her skin. The beautiful androids of L.A. weren't here. Instead, the club's clientele seemed to be made of artificial bohemians and hipsters. Clumps of bleary-faced kids with fading bleach-jobs, pierced eyebrow arches and too-skinny jeans huddled over Martini glasses and ashtrays. Lounge music (or at least an interpretation of it) squealed over the bad speaker-system.

This was not such a good idea, after all. Sheri moved away from the tables, to the center of the room. There seemed to be less smoke. She did a cursory scan of the dark club, squinting through the linoleum, haze, and black light. She turned to leave.

I'll just say that something came up... He'll understand.

"Hey, baby, I almost didn't recognize you."

French swooped down on her, nonchalantly sloshing his glowing neon drink. He stooped down and kissed her on the cheek. She smelled the alcohol on his breath, and was slightly rubbed by his five o'clock shadow. Then he unfolded himself, standing his full 6 foot 5. French's hair was still tousled. It had that just-gotten-out-of-bed look. The black dye was fading from it, with tufts of chestnut hair sticking up comically here and there. She heard the creak of his ubiquitous leather jacket.

"How you doing, sweets? Let's sit down." Sheri felt his palm touch the small of her back. She was intensely aware of it, and annoyed by it. He guided her to an empty table.

"Damn, baby, you look good. It's your hair. Don't get me wrong, I like when a Sister goes natural, but, damn, it's so silky. No more Earth Goddess look, baby?"

"Yes, I know. 'Good hair.' I can't say the same for you, though.

What's with the muttonchops? Are you auditioning for a period piece or something? And what's with the sunglasses? It's so early-80s-MTV."

"Meow, woman," he said, removing his sunglasses. French squinted at her. "You need yourself a drink. What'll it be?"

Sheri laughed, relaxing. "Something with coconut in it, with lots of rum." As she watched him head to the bar, Sheri suddenly felt that she'd made the right decision. It wouldn't be half as awkward as speaking to Darshanna. Darshanna would probably believe that she went off the Deep End, and would need Zoloft or Prozac. French, on the other hand, wouldn't care. He'd probably welcome it. They were polar opposites, French and Darshanna. Sheri met him at UCLA—both had been doing a Ph. D. program in Cultural Studies, and shared many courses together. French quit last semester, 80 pages into his thesis: *Mythisissippi: Jungian Archetypes in the Delta Blues*. When asked why, French claimed to have had a Vision, a kind of Gnostic awakening. He'd been Called to play the blues, not merely write about it in that dry, academic manner. He was now in a punk-blues band called the Sleestaks, and they played on the local scene. They even had an indie CD out—"Cozmic Sophia."

Darshanna couldn't stand him, and thought he was a fake. "How can you stand that White Negro?"

But in spite of his affectations (or maybe, *because* of them), Sheri still hung with him. He was fun, if more than a little strange.

He came back with a goblet of what looked like anti-freeze. The blue glow of the drink almost rivaled the purple shimmer of the black light.

"You are the Man," said Sheri. She tasted something with Cream of Coconut and Blue Curacao.

He stared at her for several moments. Then, he said, "What don't you tell me what this is all about."

As the alcohol and sugar sang in her blood, Sheri told him about the events of the last couple of days. During the unfolding, French didn't bat an eye; he even laughed appreciatively, as if she were speaking about obnoxious relatives instead of ghostly figures.

"...and there was a stack of pancakes, warming in the oven. And you know what I did? I *ate* them. They were the best damn pancakes I'd ever had. Light and fluffy."

" 'You add the love. Auntie Clabber does the rest,'" quoted French.

After a few moments of silence, filled by the opening bars of a Nine Inch Nails song, Sheri asked, "So...do you think I'm nuts?"

"I'm not sure—"

"What the hell does that mean? You're one to talk! After all, you quit school to play the blues, because of some mystical experience with a harp-playing blues man at a crossroads."

" Well... That's just a little exaggerated." He continued at her open-mouthed prompting. "It was a bum, playing a toy harmonica behind the Whisky. It *was* a bona fide mystical experience. Kinda."

"Uh-huh. The type of 'mystical' experience that looks good in a band's publicity kit. Darshanna's right. You're a phony. I'm outta here."

When she stood up, the room spun. Just a bit. She took a step, and the floor seemed to sink, like concrete quicksand. She'd practically guzzled her drink.

"Hey, baby, sit back down."

"Don't you 'baby' me, asshole."

"OK. Sheri, you're drunk. I forgot what a low a tolerance you had for hooch. You need to sit down." Before she could protest, he was steering her toward the seat. She sat down, sullenly.

She turned away from him. *I don't need his goddamn support. I know what I saw.*

Before she knew it, she blurted out: "You think I'm crazy, don't you? Well, screw you."

French was very calm. He sipped his drink. "I believe you," he said.

"Don't humor me."

"I'm not. Not at all. I mean, you're one of the most sane people I know. So, in spite of everything—the unreality of it all—I gotta believe you. You're kinda like a cornerstone, for me."

In spite of herself, Sheri felt herself melting. He'd taken off his dark glasses again, a gesture at once theatrical and affecting.

He cracked one of his off-center grins: "I mean, I don't *ever* recall you wearing foundation. It had to have been against your will."

They laughed.

"Come on, let me drive you home."

They wove through the throngs of postmodern hepcats, wannabe Kerouacs and Patti Smiths to the parking lot. She sat down in French's vintage aqua VW bug. As they pulled out of the Dharma Lounge's parking lot, Sheri tried not to stare at the moving plastic doll figures pasted on the dashboard—a wiggling hula girl, a Taco Bell Chihuahua, a snow globe with a mermaid floating in it. Instead, she focused on the white lines of the highway. Which didn't work either. Finally, she turned to French.

"Darshanna doesn't believe me, not one bit. She had that *look*."

French nodded: "I know the one. You know, sometimes I get that feeling that she doesn't like me very much."

"You're right. She doesn't, she calls you the White Negro." She stopped herself, and plastered her hand over her mouth. "Oops."

French only chuckled.

When they pulled into her apartment complex, it was 12:30am. A few guardian palm trees swayed in the chilly nighttime breeze.

A light was on the living room. She usually only left her bedroom light on. That was the first clue that something wasn't quite right. When she unlocked her door, the smell of syrup hit her nose immediately.

"They're here," she announced.

"Huh?" asked French. "What's that smell?"

It was sweet, cloyingly so. Sheri drank in the fumes, and her stomach began to churn.

"Show yourselves, goddammit," she said.

"I'm right here, honey chile. There ain't no reason to take de Lawd's name in vain."

The vintage poster was shimmering—the red rustle of her skirt, the pure white of her apron, the blue of her kerchief. Her skin changed from coal black crayon to something substantial, *real*. Auntie Clabber freed herself from the yellow background of the poster. As she did so, a profusion of fragrance followed her—heralding her metamorphosis.

Maple syrup, hot butter, vanilla.

"Fuck," said French.

The odor was so intense (and she was so drunk and sleep-deprived), that Sheri's stomach began to churn in violent reaction. The thought of eating gave rise to a thousand phantom flapjacks crawling around in her stomach. She felt them climbing up into throat, splashing the back of her tongue with the incongruous taste of coconut spiked with bitter bile. Sheri ran to the bathroom, both trying to keep her balance and quell the geyser within.

She knelt by the toilet, and lifted up its lid. She became a dragon then, breathing fire. For a while all was liquid and confusion. She felt someone touching the small of her back, stroking it gently. She heard singing, a gospel-tinged voice, between her heaves. When Sheri finished vomiting, she rested her head against the cool porcelain.

"I think she'll be jes fine," she heard Auntie Clabber say. "Help me get her onto a couch. She needs her rest."

She wanted to say, 'Don't touch me,' but she was too weak. The two of them stood her up, and walked her back to the living room, and deposited her on the couch. Auntie Clabber produced a cup of strong black coffee—perhaps magically. Sheri didn't remember having any more coffee in the house. The fumes cleared her head. French placed a can of ginger ale in front of her. She sipped it cautiously, feeling the burn of spice and carbonation traveling down her throat to settle in her stomach. She lay back on the couch after she finished half the soda and closed her eyes. She overheard the two of them speaking over her:

"It jes ain't right. She shouldna been drinkin. That stuff's a demon's drink. Hit's poison. A young lady like her shouldn't be drinkin. It jes ain't right." Auntie Clabber tsked and tutted over her, adjusting pillows underneath her head.

"Listen, you obnoxious cartoon character—" Sheri started. She kept her eyes closed. She didn't even want to see the bumbling mammy.

French interrupted her: "Sheri, stop. You know that when she was—*created*, it wasn't soon after Prohibition."

"I don't 'preciate you talking bout me, when I'm right here," said

Auntie Clabber. "Ain't like I'm deaf and dumb."

"I'm sorry. It's just... I mean, you're alive. You were in that poster, and now you're here. It's strange." French paused. "What's it like, being in there."

Auntie Clabber sat down on the arm of the couch; Sheri could feel the rustle of her petticoats. "I... I jes don't rightly know."

"Do you remember anything?"

"Yes. No. Cain't really say." Her voice drifted. She stood up suddenly. "Would you like something to eat? You looks awful thin."

Sheri could hear her stomping to the kitchen.

French knelt by her: "She's fucking amazing. A walking semiotic, a simulacrum, come to life..."

Sheri managed to open her eyes. "Yeah. Amazing." She rubbed her temples. "Say, she didn't seem too keen on your line of questioning, about her existence as a piece of paper."

French nodded. "She just seemed to shut down."

"Reverted to her natural state. She's hardwired: stereotypical folk aphorisms and delicious pancakes. She's a robot—a Stepford Negro."

"She's more than that, don't you think? I mean, she's a new life form... Just think about the possibilities. What were the others like—Lula and Beulah?"

Sheri sat up, and took a swig of ginger ale. It had lost a little of its fizz. "They were different." She went on, in response to his prompting glances: "They're creepy. They seem more aware of what they're doing. And they're sneaky. I mean Auntie Clabber is a little annoying, but Lula is... She's crafty. I don't like the other two at all. I mean, *look* at me!"

French humphed in agreement. "I wonder if any other characters are going to come to life. Like Uncle Ben. Or Huckleberry Hound..."

"Screw that. What I want—what I *need* to know is how they came to life? And why."

"When faced with the miraculous, it's best just to enjoy it, and not fuck it up by asking why."

"Easier said than done."

French glanced toward the kitchen. "Let's look at this logically, then. What's the one constant in these...manifestations?"

Sheri leaned toward him. "They're all objects that I'm studying for my thesis—"

"That's not where I was going with this. The one constant is *you*. They hang around you. So it's a reasonable assumption that you have some kinda power—"

"OK. All right. It's time for you to go." Sheri stood up, and gave French a friendly but firm shove. "It's hard enough to deal with all of this stuff. But to have you talking about my 'hidden powers' just puts it over the top."

French unfolded; with his head barely clearing the ceiling, he was nearly as surreal as the advertisement ladies. Sheri unlocked the door and gestured him outside. She was beginning to feel a deep-down weariness. It affected her eyesight, blurring everything outside to a blobbish sepia.

"I'll call you," he said. He bent down and kissed her lightly on the cheek. She closed the door after him.

"Aren't you glad that we dolled you up? You just landed yourself a man."

Sheri spun around, and saw Beulah and Lula, flickering in television tones. Beulah had been the speaker; she was smiling like a cat that has just eaten a bird. Sheri was hit with a wave of lye and lavender.

"Not just any man," Lula purred, "but a *white* man. Let me work with your skin, darling, and I'll make him a keeper. You'll no longer be his little pet African; you can be his wife. If anyone can make you pass, I can."

"And let me work some more with your hair. I'll turn that greasy, black bush of yours into a waterfall of curly tresses, as soft as velvet."

Their forms settled and stopped shimmering. They began advancing on her, like they had the first time she'd seen them.

"Go away." Sheri didn't have any strength or will left.

The two ghost-women grabbed her and led her to the sofa, ignoring her protests. She felt their nails piercing her. Nails. Claws. Like cats.

They started grooming her, with their perfumes and poisons. "Please, stop."

"Aw, now darling," whispered Lula, stroking her face tenderly, "just relax. Everything will be fine."

Beulah was the bad cop: "I just don't understand; we're gonna help you to get a white man, for free, and all we get is disrespect."

"Leave her alone." Auntie Clabber's voice cut through their sensual jabbering like a hot knife through butter.

The two women stopped their ministrations, and turned their heads towards Auntie simultaneously. They looked at each other; a message seemed to pass through them—they *shimmered* in agreement. Apparently, they decided to ignore the old icon. Lula's lavender was wafting up to her, tickling her nose.

"I done said, leave the girl chile alone."

Beulah paused; she had a strand of Sheri's hair in her hand; she could feel it melting in the lye-scented heat of her hand.

"Don't make me have ta tell you again." Auntie Clabber's voice was firm. When Lula and Beulah parted, Sheri got a clear view of her. Her hands were on her hips, her black face wrinkled with rage, her black eyes spitting daggers. There was something primeval about her, then. She was already supernatural, like a cartoon character. Now she was supernatural, as in a force of nature personified.

"Now, listen here—" started Beulah.

Lula interrupted her: "No, darling, let me handle this. Auntie Clabber, sweet l'il thing, why don't you go back in the kitchen and do what you do best? You make the world's lightest, airiest pancakes. So tender and buttery—why, they bring tears to my eyes! It's what you were made for, darling. Why don't you let us do what we were made for—to turn this wild child of the jungle into a sophisticated lady of the city."

"Well, when you put it thataway, Miz Lula," started Auntie Clabber, "I jest gotta say, Hell no!"

Lula was taken aback. She sat down on the couch. She pulsed, from black and white to Technicolor. Beulah flashed in response. The seductress was defeated. It was time for Bad Cop to have a go at it.

"Listen here, you flapjack flipping Tar Baby, you go back to wherever it is you came from, and let us do our work!"

Auntie Clabber stomped over to Beulah, who suddenly seemed very frail in her wispy white gown next to Auntie Clabber's considerable girth, clothed in warpaint red.

"I don't wanna hear no more mess from you, Missy. I don't understand myself why she don't wanna be beautified and all, but I *does* know that she don't wanna be messed with. And that's all I needs to know. So quit messing with her, if you know what's good for you."

"Now, Auntie Darling—"

"Now don't you be tryin them sugar words on me."

The Lightening Cream lady blanched. The Lye Queen began to wilt, like so much hair under a hot comb. Sentence should read: The two of them carefully withdrew from the couch.

Sheri's head was clear, and she was over the shock of Auntie Clabber's anger. She took advantage of the situation.

"I want you two to leave me alone," she said. Her voice faltered. "And never come back here again."

"Anything you say, darling. You know, we were only trying to help..."

Beulah muttered something under her breath.

"What was that?" Auntie Clabber perked up.

"I said, you gotta sleep sometime, girl. Don't know what's good for you..."

Clabber cut her off. She purposefully walked up to the two ladies, and grabbed their wispy dresses' necks. She hefted them off the ground. The two of them struggled like reluctant cats. They began to slash at Clabber with their manicured nails. Hairline fractures appeared on Clabber's face and arms. Blood trickled, syrup-thick; but Clabber didn't seem to mind. She dragged them in front of a blank poster, which promptly began to pulse and throb. First she hurled Beulah into the vertical lake of white; Lula quickly followed her in. There was a moment in which the two of them screamed in fury. Then the puddling of the poster stopped. Their horrible faces were frozen against a beige background.

Sheri was mesmerized by the fear and rage expressed by the Lye Queen and the Lightening Queen; it was like some parody of a vintage poster.

"Quick, chile!" Auntie Clabber's urgency shook her out of the trance. "You gotta get rid of that poster, or they'll be back."

Sheri nodded. She walked up to the poster, and tore it down. She crumbled it up. She felt some kind of weird resistance. It was silky beneath her hands. Then it became slimy, a parchment smeared with snot and snail goo. She almost dropped it. Sheri heard faint voices, slithery, feline, cartoon voices. She tore off one corner of the poster. A scream, felt rather than heard, vibrated through her body. She tore a whole length off. A noxious odor arose and overpowered her, at once cloying and revolting. It brought tears to her eyes.

She tore the poster into a hundred shreds, until the cloud of mingled lavender and lye dissipated. Sheri began gathering up the demon confetti, and threw it into the trashcan in the kitchen. Auntie Clabber helped her, by sweeping up the trash with a broom. After every last trace of them had been banished from the apartment, the two of them sat down on the couch. Sheri felt drained.

"Lordy, lordy," sighed Auntie Clabber.

Sheri looked at her. Her face had healed, but a few stray strands of hair had escaped from her kerchief. She was sweating and winded.

Her whole life has been dedicated to working, to catering to other people's needs, Sheri thought. *I feel sorry for her.* She paused in mid-thought: *Wait a second! She's just a damned cartoon character, a phantasm...*

"Thanks," said Sheri quickly, afraid that she'd go back to rationalizing the events of the last few days as the delusions of an overworked grad student. "You really stuck up for me."

"Aw, shucks," Clabber beamed. Her face broke out into a thousand embarrassed wrinkles, each of them smiling at her. The light burnished her skin, bought out the subtle warm tones in her skin. "T'weren't nothing."

She stood up. "Well, I guess it's time for me to go back." She headed for a blank poster on the wall. "I promises not to worry you no more."

"Where are you going?"

"Don't you go fretting 'bout Auntie Clabber; she can take care of herself." She paused momentarily. "I won't come to see you, I mean that. I jes hope I'm not as annoying as them two heifers."

Sheri was horrified: "No, don't you even think that. I... You never answered that question, that French had. What's it like in there?"

Clabber paused for a long moment. Her face was serious, frozen. She said: "It's like nothing. Breathing, but there ain't no air. Flowers, but there ain't no smell. Water, but there ain't no wet. It ain't never hot, nor cold. It's like being asleep, 'cept you don't never get no rest. But don't you worry bout me. I'll be jes fine. I been there all my life."

Before she knew what she was saying, it was out of her mouth: "You're not going back in there. No. It sounds—horrible. Like you are some kind of psychic puppet or something. No. You're not going back."

Something like fear bloomed in Clabber's eyes. "Is you sure, chile?"

"I'm sure."

The fear was still in Clabber's eyes.

"You can stay here," Sheri prompted. "We'll figure something out, but later. At least until after I finish my thesis." Sheri jumped up: "You can sleep on the couch. It folds out into a bed. It's actually quite comfortable... What is it?"

Auntie Clabber unfroze from her statue-still stance, and glanced at Sheri.

"It's jest... What do I do? Ain't never really been Outside."

Sheri sighed, and walked over to the large woman in crimson. She hugged her. "I don't know," she said, "you'll just have to find out."

Auntie Clabber whispered, "I don't even know who I am..."

"So, girl, don't keep me in suspense. What did La Bouche have to say about your first draft?" Darshanna had barged in minutes after she'd come in from her meeting. She wore a navy-blue and white patterned batik ensemble, with ankh earrings. She had just put on the kettle to boil. It now whistled.

"Let me turn off the pot. You want some tea?"

"Screw that. Tell me what happened?"

"Just one damn minute!"

Sheri left her in the living room, while she poured herself a cup of jasmine tea. She walked back to the living room, sipping the hot liquid. She sat on the chair; Darshanna had enthroned herself on the couch.

"Well," she started as she put down her mug on the coffee table, "as to be expected, La Bouche was in an awful mood. She had just gotten out of meeting with another grad student, and apparently it didn't go well. I'd been standing outside of the door, and heard her walking stick nearly cracking the floor. I swear, she's worse than a 5.2 on the Richter scale. So I went in, kind of nervous. Like she's gonna rip me a new one. But at the same time, I'm *not* scared. I'm beyond fear. Cause, you know, I took some risks with the text. Big risks." Sheri gulped more tea, fully aware that Darshanna was literally on the edge of her seat. "So, I sit down, dutiful student in front of her majesty.

"And, true to form, Bouchier goes for the jugular: 'Ms. Alexander, you seem awfully full of yourself. You're smiling, like an exceptionally pleased cat. I hate the horrid beasts. Perhaps you can tell me why you're beaming?'

"I gathered up my courage, and said to her, 'Because I don't give a fuck, pardon my French. I know it's the best thing that I've written.'

"'Ms. Alexander, you're bordering on the arrogant.' La Bouche tapped her walking stick on the floor. 'But, you arrogant little shit, you're quite right. Oh, there are some rough spots here and there, and you'll see that I've painted your manuscript with notes. But it kept me riveted. The mixture of fiction and theory was unique, engaging, and learned. You clearly know what you're talking about. By giving these advertising images of the African American voice and character, you definitely bring to light the ideology that hides behind them. And the daring complexity—Auntie Clabber as both nurturing mammy, and nascent Earth-mother—half developed, but intriguing!'"

"You go, girl!" Darshanna clapped.

Just then, the door to her apartment opened.

Darshanna turned to see who was entering.

"Darshanna, I want you to meet my new roommate, Annie Clabbert."

For a second, Darshanna looked as if she was going to laugh. But she thought better of it. But her eyes were wide with recognition and disbelief.

She shook Clabber's hand. Clabber was wearing dark jeans, Doc Martens, and a t-shirt that read CAUTION: EDUCATED BLACK WOMAN.

"Pleased to meet you. Sheri here done told me about you."

"Um, yes. Likewise."

"Sheri, chile, how did your meeting go?"

"Wonderfully. I can now call La Bouche by her first name. I am officially apart of Laetitia's inner circle."

"Congratulations. How was rehearsal?"

Clabber shook her head: "That French is something else, ain't he? He wants me to do some lead vocals on some of the songs."

"Well, congratulations to you." Sheri hugged the older woman.

Darshanna interrupted them. "Let's go out. My treat. To celebrate Sheri's ascension to favored student."

"I couldn't..." started Sheri.

"I insist. It'll be nothing fancy. And besides, I've had a craving for good, greasy diner food. I'll take you all to Roscoe's House of Chicken and Waffles."

"You girls go on ahead. I've got to memorize some new material for the Sleestaks. And besides, I jest hate pancakes! Can't even stand the smell of 'em!"

Clabber winked at Sheri before she disappeared into the kitchen.

Conjuring Shadows

Silhouette
On the face of the moon
Am I.
A dark shadow in the light.
A silhouette am I
On the face of the moon
Lacking color
Or vivid brightness
But defined all the clearer
Because
I am dark,
Black on the face of the moon.
A shadow am I
Growing in the light,
Not understood as is the day,
But more easily seen
Because
I am a shadow in the light.
—"Shadow," by Richard Bruce Nugent (1925)

Mrs. Alberta Dufrense's collection of Harlem Renaissance era art is small but impressive. She has a William Johnson piece, a sketch by Jacob Lawrence, and a maquette by Augusta Savage. Lesser known artists are included, along with a smattering a of first edition volumes (Van Vetchen's *Nigger Heaven*, Hurston's *Of Mules and Men*) and a file cabinet of correspondence. The collection is housed in the library of her Washington, DC home, which is situated in the newly revitalized Logan Circle area. Mrs. Dufrense has lent out pieces of her collection to various traveling exhibits and museums in addition to providing (by appointment only) access to curious visitors and scholars. But there is one piece she has that never leaves her collection. In fact, it is not even properly a part of collection, as she has sequestered it in her bedroom.

"Empress" rests on her bed's headboard. At first glance, it appears to be some kind of Art Deco vase. It's a smooth black oblong, about the size of an infant. The surface is scored with double lines, like seams. The sculpture rests on "feet" and elongated "arms," as if it is kneeling in a supplicant's pose. The front of the piece has three faint indentations—eyes, a mouth—that suggest a face. "Empress" suggests form, even as it blurs the distinction between the abstract and the representational.

The material that "Empress" is made of is as intriguing as the piece itself. Neither clay nor stone nor metal, it seems to have all of their qualities. The glaze is a kind of *living* blackness that shimmers. Even when there is no light—as Mrs. Dufrense graciously demonstrated when she turned the light off in her bedroom—the piece pulsates. The form stands out in low light. The supplicant's shape seems to absorb what ever light there is, and radiate it out. It is does not shine; there is no spectrum. Only a void.

The feel of the piece is warm and smooth. Even soft, like the fur of some animal. And—

"Can you feel it?" asks Mrs. Dufrense. "There's a pulse there. A *heartbeat.*"

Not much is known about the artist, Courtney Vaughan (1898-1961). He was raised in North Carolina. Attended Howard University, where he was mentored by Augusta Savage, and socialized with Langston Hughes and Zora Hurston. Most of his work is representational, reflecting the Great Migration, and while technically proficient, is not particularly of note. The only thing that survives of his papers is a widely anthologized piece of short fiction that captures the zeitgeist of 1920s Harlem and the life of black homosexuals in that era.

Temple Cats
By Courtney Vaughan

Midnight in Darkytown. All the decent folks are asleep, safe in

God's loving arms. But we others, the prodigal sons, we never sleep. We roam the neon night, restless with sin. There is an alley, a normal alley haunted by laundry floating on lines like ghosts. Cats prowl in garbage, risking all nine of their lives. We're bigger cats in zootsuits, who sneak in hidden nooks and corners, smoking catnip and tobacco. Silken cresses, konked hair, swishing tails. All of us converge around a door in the alley. The basement of an apartment building with a door the color of wine. One by one, we go to the door. We knock. An viewhole opens. A password is whispered, the door opens. Light and music spill out, only to be shut again. What is behind the door?

Down the marble steps, we enter the Temple. The floor is black and white, like a chessboard. Rugs with geometric designs interrupt the tiles. Potted palms sway in fan-stirred air. The wallpaper has hieroglyphics on it, men and women with the heads of beasts. Column lintels are encrusted with blue and green stones. An oud rests against one wall; a stuffed peacock, tail in a full fan, glares from another. A bar with illicit hard liquor beckons while on a dais a trio of upright bass, cocktail drum, and trumpet plays. The smell of incense curls around the floor, and good, clean tobacco. But this elaborate set up is not why we are here, not most of us, anyway.

We are here for this: Men, in darker hues, who dance the dance of the Prodigal. The kiss, the caress, the flirt. The thing that can never be seen in the world of Above. Masks are removed, mannerisms relaxed. In the Temple, we are free to worship the flesh, away from judging eyes. Here, we are free from euphemism, conjecture, scandal and gossip. We whisper our secrets. Deals and rendezvous are made in shadowed corners. We are safe here. We temple cats weave and purr in the subterranean basement, attuned to the rhythms of night, jazz, and, yes, the sacred.

An hour passes, two. Spirits are imbibed, as are kisses. Gradually, silence descends. We pause, and glance at the stage. The musicians have stopped playing. The bass lies on its side like a woman laying down. And a woman emerges from the shadows. A giantess, her hips and breasts shaped like the bass. And she's strung with a sheer white gown that floats on her ebony body. It's belted at the waist with the golden snake of a belt. Her muscled arms are bare. Her hair is hidden by an elaborate white headdress made of horn, shells and feathers that glow. We gasp and sigh in wonder—she is the goddess-empress of this domain. She steps up to the lip of the stage. In her nacre heels with silver straps and her headdress, she stands nearly eight feet tall.

"Greetings, my children," she says, extending her arms out in a gesture of welcome that holds all of us to her. We thrill at the sound of her voice—that rich, deep contralto. And we *are* her children. We gather closer, eager for what is to come.

The bassist comes and stands his instrument up, and begins to pluck notes from it. The Goddess-Empress begins to recite poetry in a foreign tongue. Both sounds bounce off the walls of the Temple. It's a wild, mad journey through sound. This, indeed, is our church, and she shout-sings the words like gospel hymns. Shouts of "praise be!" rises from the audience. One cat in a charcoal gray suit swoons. And claps and stomps his feet in some religious mania. The poem ends with a yell that echoes through the Temple. The trumpeter takes up his golden horn and sends out a moan, and she recites another poem, this one in English. Her cadence and phrasing is beautiful. Do a few cheeks glisten with tears? Perhaps. She smiles at us, her faithful congregation. The music plays on. But before she leaves the stage to mingle with the masses, she blows a kiss out to us.

The kiss, that collection of darkness and breath, flows through us. Each of us feels the moist tingle of lips on our throats, the atoms of the Goddess-Empress's breath. It is warm. It's a mother's kiss; more. It's both sacred and profane—much like our midnight love. And that is the color of the kiss, the breath—midnight. It's a tangible thing, this expelled breath. It roams the Temple. It soars in the ceiling, bouncing from the draperies that depend from the rafters, a bird of shadow. It circles the pillars, an asp of shade. It prowls the checkered floor, panther-like.

We return to our various coteries after having been blessed by her Kiss. Drinks flow. Cigarette smoke rises. Music swells. And kisses begin to fall like rain—

A ferocious pounding on the door interrupts the sway of things.

The music stops, as does the chatter. The doorman opens the viewhole. There's an aggressive exchange between the outside and the doorman.

"It's the police, ya'll!"

We tense, ready to flee. But it is hopeless. Where is there to go? We only know of the one entrance. The doorman looks to the Goddess-Empress.

"Let them in," she says.

The door is unlocked, and in they flow, boys in blue, clubs and guns drawn. One of them, a tall brute of a fellow with mustache like a comb says in a booming voice: "Police! You are all under arrest, for unlawful and immoral congregation, according to the Decency code..." We listen to him rattle off boilerplate legalese. We cease to coalesce; the wreckage of destroyed careers and families looms in front of us.

When the lead officer finishes his speech, the Goddess-Empress proudly parts the masses that throng around her. She towers over him, in her ivory gown and baroque headdress.

"Officer," she says in her dark honey voice, "I am sure that we can come to an arrangement."

The officer steps back suddenly, almost as if she'd attacked him. Another steps forward, and cracks her across the cheek. The Goddess-Empress stumbles. Her headdress teeters, then crashes to the floor. And she is revealed. She is bald, and beneath the garish makeup are the features of a man. Blood drips on her creamy white gown. One of the cops laughs. Another murmurs, "freak."

The Goddess-Empress raises her noble head, gestures and—

The Kiss, that substance made of breath and darkness rises. It is a sphere of black. It rises until it hangs over us all, police and criminals. Our eyes are transfixed. The Kiss *eats* our vision. Someone yells, "What the hell is that thing?" A gunshot is fired, right into the heart of the sphere. The bullet is absorbed with barely the hint of a ripple. The Kiss roams over the crowd. Those beneath its shadow begin to paw each other. We begin to kiss each other. The police are absorbed into us as they are touched by the Kiss's shadow, and they, too, begin to kiss. Clothes and uniforms fly off. Flesh touches flesh. Fingers, lips and other things find each other.

We become temple cats, all of us.

The Goddess-Empress calmly restores her headdress to its rightful place. She weaves between the couples, and dims the Temple's lights.

Some rituals are meant for darkness. (*1926*)

While Vaughn's piece is undoubtedly a piece of florid fantasia, there are oblique references to events, places and even persons in Harlem Renaissance in New York. For instance, there *was* a underground speakeasy in Harlem, a known hang out for gay black men, called Timbuktu. Rather than a fixed location, this was a party that drifted from apartment to basement to abandoned hall, protected by passwords—known in the parlance of then as '*charms*'—to avoid the unwelcome attention of the police. Timbuktu managed to avoid the Prohibition and Decency raids for quite while, but there is a record of at least one such unfortunate event that ruined many reputations.

The Goddess-Empress character closely—but not completely—resembles a personage that frequented both the art world and black gay scene, known as Madame Isis. She is mentioned here and there: a statuesque and theatrical woman who skirted around the edges of these milieus. Reports, cobbled together from letters and interviews claim that she was a wealthy patron of the arts. Other denizens believe that she was a kind of a literal madame, with her specialty clientele being men "in the life." Some thought that she was just a meddlesome fag hag, while others believed that she had Sapphic inclinations herself and lived vicariously through the lives of her ubiquitous coterie. Vaughn's tale is not the only one that casts her as a transgender person. Wilder rumors have her connected to the mob, and some claim that she was some kind of conjure-woman, trained in the arts of *obeah*. All accounts claim that she was a giantess.

No image of her survives.

Zora's Destiny

They said she could pull lightning bolts right outta the sky and play them like guitar strings. They said, cats would sing and dance at her command. They said the Man in the Moon and B'rer Rabbit and B'rer Fox were all her gentleman callers, and they competed with each other for her affections.

Zora, however, had her doubts. For one thing, Miss Hattie lived in a shack. It was a perfectly nice shack, painted a gay, pinkish color, like the inside of a grapefruit. But it still was a shack. And why would someone as powerful as The Man in the Moon visit Hattie when he could have a princess? Another thing: she didn't see haints fluttering around her garden, like that Duke boy said; nor did any of the plants scream like bloody murder when she brushed by them, like Sukie Watkins claimed. Still, she'd be cautious. She would do her Mama no good ending up dead, or in a witch's stew pot.

Zora had made the plan to visit Hattie earlier that day, in the afternoon, at the general store. Papa'd sent her there for more headache powders. She didn't know why; the headache powder didn't seem to ease Mama's ailment any. It'd been three days since Mama had her spells. Mama described the pain in truly frightening terms. Zora overheard them speaking one night. Mama's voice was as coarse as cornmeal, hard and dry.

"It's like there are a thousand living needles in my head, each of them glowing red with heat. If I move—if there's too much light—they wake up and stab my brain. Even seeing things hurt. Seeing things cause things to shatter, hairline cracks..."

Papa had tried to say some soothing things to her, but it was no use. Zora thought that maybe he sent her out just to be away from Mama's illness. That's when she overheard Xenia Mae White talking to the

Widow Ferguson about Hattie's healing abilities.

The Widow Ferguson was wearing her customary black. She'd been a widow longer than she'd been married, and she seemed to like the role and clothing. She said, "Sister White, I swear that woman is godless—a heathen. But she sure knows how to take away pain. You might want to visit her, next time the curse reckons to visit you."

"I don't know. Chester wouldn't like it, not one bit. He says that she consorts with old world devils. That's where she gets her power." Xenia Mae White was tall and thin as a willow branch. She had a high yellow complexion and soft curls. She hailed from New Orleans and still had a faint accent.

The Widow Ferguson harumphed. "Men don't know everything. Some of them old ways are good, better than the new ones."

"But...your soul. Doesn't the Good Book say we shouldn't suffer a witch to live?"

The Widow Ferguson waved the notion away. "You know I have rheumatism real bad? Well, I went to her. She simply touched my arm." Here, she demonstrated, by grabbing a hold of Xenia Mae White's forearm. "And the pain just leeched away. I swear, I could see the pain creep away, like an army of fire ants underneath my skin, and swarm up her arm. There, they faded away. She killed my pain! Then she gave me some pretty nasty looking elixir and told me to drink it every night. And you know, my joints don't ache anymore?"

Mrs. White shivered at the description of the fire ants; she was thoroughly scandalized. The two women went on through the store, talking about other things, mostly church gossip. By this time, Zora already had the headache powder. She waited until the women left the store, and parted, Mrs. White going to the right, the Widow Ferguson to the left. Zora ran after the woman.

"Mrs. Ferguson!"

The woman turned. "Hello, child. Ain't you one of Rev Hurston's children? Don't you look pretty?"

Zora remembered to thank her, and barreled on: "I overheard you at the general store, talking with Mrs. White, about Hattie. Do you know where she lives?"

The Widow Ferguson frowned at her. She probably came from the old-fashioned school of thought that children, particularly, girl-children, should be seen and not heard. Zora didn't have time for that mess.

"Child, what's your name?"

"Sarah," Zora lied. Let her sainted sister get in trouble, for once.

"Sarah, you know it's rude to eavesdrop. Not ladylike at all. I know your folks taught you better than that!"

Zora looked at the ground, and pretended to be suitably chastised. She waited, as the widow looked her over, as if she were trying to suss out her agenda.

"Why do you want to know, Sarah?"

Zora kept her eyes trained on the ground before her. "You see, my mama's real sick. Has been for over three days...." The acting part ended abruptly. The tears that spilled from her eyes were real, and rose from the well in her heart. Mama was her best friend in the whole wide world. If Papa was granite-hard and cold, Mama was soft as a feather and warm. Her sister Sarah was the apple of Papa's eye. To him, Zora was an afterthought, the girl who wasn't Sarah. But Mama always made Zora feel special. She encouraged her. Papa just thought she was a bad liar with an overactive imagination. "Why can't you be more respectful, like your sister?" he'd ask her. But Mama saw good things in Zora: "You have an indomitable spirit. And you're quite a storyteller. Jump at the sun, my darling, jump at the sun!" Zora couldn't imagine what life would be like without Mama there. She wished that she were sick in Mama's place. She was nothing; Mama was an angel sent from God.

Before she knew it, the Widow Ferguson had pressed Zora to her ample bosom. All Zora could see was the warp and weft of black fabric. She heard the widow's heart beat beneath, and smelled the sweet lavender scent of her toilet water, which was the same that Mama wore.

"Oh, child," said the widow. She stroked her head. "It's against my better judgment. But I'll tell you. Hattie lives at the very end of Oleander Road, on the west side of town. I can't imagine your daddy agreeing to see her, on a count of him being a man of God. But, desperate times call for desperate measures, I suppose." She gave Zora an extra squeeze, and released her. "Godspeed, Sarah. Your mama, Miss Lucy, is real sweet. I hope that Hattie can help her!"

It was evening by the time she wandered down winding Oleander Road. It had taken a while to find it, and even longer to walk it. Pavement changed to dust roads. Fancy houses with gardens and picket fences turned into broken down shacks. Once, she was chased down the road a spell by mean looking mutt before the owner, a cross-eyed man, called the beast back. She passed a group of musicians sitting on a porch, setting up their instruments for an evening show: guitar, washboard, and jug. The men waved at her; she recognized one of them: Otis Byrne. He was a handyman and he'd once repaired a leaky roof. When she saw him, she made sure that she looked like she knew where she was going by putting an extra spring in her step.

Now that she was finally here, she was cowed. She realized that she had no money to offer the conjure woman. And how was she gonna get her to visit Mama and pull the pain out of her head? There was a distant rumble of thunder. Zora looked up to see fat gray clouds gathering on the horizon, and could smell the rain in the air.

Great. Her dress would be ruined, and Papa would surely tan her hide. She would have to think of that later. The pink shack had a porch, but no overhang. She ran up the rickety stairs, and pounded on the door. No answer.

Then: she heard a voice. It came from around the corner, at the back of the house. The voice was dark and muddy, like a creek. It sounded like stones buried deep beneath the silt and the roots of trees, and other secret places underground. It sang no words that Zora knew; maybe the stones and the roots knew the language. Whatever words were being sung, they were sweet, rich and melodious, musical molasses. Zora followed the sound of the voice to the back.

In the yard, in the middle of a wild garden full of pungent herbs, stood the tallest woman Zora had ever seen. She must have been six feet, at least. She wore a man's overalls and her hair was unprocessed and white as the full moon. Her eyes were closed, as if she were concentrating on the notes that came from her mouth.

So, this was Hattie. Zora had seen her before, around Eatonville. She'd always assumed she was a he, a strange elderly man. The song on went for a while. Fireflies crept out of their hiding places and surrounded Hattie with a halo of winking light. The crickets, frogs and cicadas seemed to stop their own songs, giving space to the unfurling dark song. Hattie was directing her voice upwards, to the sky. Zora glanced up and she saw that there was a perfect circle of sky in the cloud cover, and the circle was widening. Thunder rumbled and lighting flickered, white and violet. Rain fell down in torrents, yet she and Hattie—her garden and her house—were dry. The sky-circle spread, and the first of the evening stars were visible against the robin's egg-blue of the sky.

That was when Zora became aware of the power thrumming through the song. She felt it, the song of roots and river stones, in her bones. And at the moment of her awareness, Hattie stopped singing.

Silence.

Then Hattie turned slowly, and nonchalantly said, "Come in, child. Have some tea, and tell me what you came for."

Zora shivered. In a way, this was scarier than what either Sukie or that Duke boy had told her. Sinister plants and supernatural boyfriends, she knew how to react to. (She would've run away, lickety-split). But, being invited into a hoodoo's lair—that was a little trickier. How could she refuse?

"Yes, ma'am," Zora said, after a pause.

Hattie picked up a basket filled with various herbs, and walked in the house. She held the door for Zora, waiting for her to enter. Zora reluctantly did so. Maybe this was a bad idea, she thought. No-one knew where she was. Except, the Widow Ferguson and Otis Byrne. But neither of them could get word to her folks in time, should anything happen.

Any foreboding she had entering the pink shack was forgotten as soon as she stepped over the threshold. Fear was overpowered by wonder. There were no books here, but it was like a small library was in this shack all the same. Things hung from every available rafter and hook on the wall: chandeliers made of dried herbs, flowers, animal pelts and other things, like bird claws. There were mason jars everywhere, full of strange liquids in different colors—urine yellow and tar black. One jar held the eyeballs of some tiny creature, perhaps a lizard; the eyes were yellow and bisected with a black slit. Another held down feathers, while yet another had some kind of creature suspended in an opaque, brownish liquid. The whole room smelled of chemicals, musk, perfume and rot. It made Zora's skin crawl, and at the same time, her curiosity stirred, like Sis Cat's fatal flaw.

"Have a seat," said Hattie. She swept a chair clean of whatever dust was on it. Zora obeyed. What else could she do, in the presence of such power? Sitting in the chair across from her, was a large marmalade tabby. It stared at her intensely, as if it were figuring her out. It was disconcerting, to say the least. Zora had the feeling that *cat* was one of its temporary forms.

Hattie rattled the chair. "Move along, Teacake," she told the monster cat, and it lazily shrugged and hopped down to the floor. Teacake sauntered over to the foot of the wood-burning stove. He sat sphinx-like, and his green gaze never left Zora. She shivered. Maybe Papa was right, about her being headstrong to the point of foolishness. Maybe she should strive to be more like Saint Sarah.

Hattie laughed, "Don't mind him. He just looks intimidating. He's just a big ole sweetheart."

Zora smiled, while she thought to herself, *I'm not so sure about that.*

Hattie busied herself with stuffing a pipe with tobacco—something that was most decidedly not ladylike. But she was not here to give the conjure woman comportment lessons; she was here on an important mission.

"My mama," Zora began. And suddenly, like when she was with the Widow Ferguson, she was overcome with emotion. She tamped it down, continued. "My mama. She real sick. Her head aches so bad, she can't see straight. Even laying in bed don't do no good for her."

Hattie puffed on her pipe, sent an amorphous shape into the air. "Is that so," she said.

80

"Do you know what's wrong with her?" Zora asked. Her grief paused, mostly because she was kind of shocked at Hattie's distant demeanor. They could've been talking about eggs, or the weather.

"Could be a lot of things," Hattie replied slowly. "I'd have to see her."

"Oh, no! I mean, that's not possible." *Because Papa would denounce you as a witch*, she thought. "I mean, do you have something, some medicine that I can take back home...."

Hattie set down her pipe. The smoke curled and formed a gauzy screen that she gazed through. Her brown eyes were inscrutable, and as unsettling as the cat's glare.

"Child," she said, in a voice weathered by smoke and moonshine, "half a conjure woman's power comes from those who believe in her. If I had your ma in front of me, I could draw the pain right from her, but only if she let me."

"But," Zora said quietly, "I saw you sing the rain and thunder away. I saw it with my own eyes."

Hattie laughed; it was a bitter sound, without humor. "You saw, and you *believed*. Not everyone can do that." She sighed, and took up the pipe again.

Zora looked at the filthy floor. It probably hadn't been swept in... forever. She saw the cracks in the wall—the shack was rickety, liable to fall down any moment. A sneeze could raze the house. So. Hattie was fake. There were no powers. And Teacake, as big as he was, was only a cat, after all. Zora looked up, and heard the patter of rain on the roof.

Papa's fire-and-brimstone tirades against Hoodoo floated to the top of her mind. On the road to Eatonville, they'd stopped in an all Negro town in Alabama. Everywhere, on the outskirts, on poles and glued to walls, were signs advertising Professor Zeke's Miracle Tonic. The posters featured a smiling gentleman holding a bottle with ornate script. Miracle Tonic, according to what her sister Sarah read to her, could cure all ills, like rheumatism, headaches and toothaches. It aided in digestion, and helped the blood circulate. Papa told Sarah to be quiet and to stop reading that "heathenish" stuff. Sarah, of course, obeyed, but Zora was fascinated by posters, that had images of snakes, and plants—things that were apparently, ingredients in this tonic. Later that evening, they had dinner in the town restaurant, a real treat. The food wasn't as good as Mama's, but Zora had felt all grown-up, sitting at a table surrounded by other customers and being served, as if she were a princess. The stately dining room, with its purple damask wall paper, however, plunged into a flurry of activity when Professor Zeke himself entered the establishment.

Professor Zeke was a portly fellow, dressed in bright red slacks held up by suspenders, a black shirt, and red shoes. He wore an Indian chief's headdress of eagle feathers on his bald, brown head. He was accompanied by three or four women who followed him, and waited on him, hand and foot, folding napkins, pulling out a chair for him, even mopping his brow. The Hurston family watched as Professor Zeke ordered a feast: mountains of mashed potatoes swimming in oceans of gravy, a hen house full of fried chickens, a bakery's worth of piping hot biscuits. Their server, a young woman who could have been no more than sixteen, practically swooned when she saw him.

"I heard that he came here every now and then!" she said. "I hear he sometimes gives folks free samples of the Miracle Tonic, if you're nice to him."

Her father grumbled. "He's a false prophet, if you ask me. Cheating honest folks out of their hard-earned cash money."

Mama looked slightly—embarrassed? Zora wasn't sure. The waitress, however, was scandalized. "Oh no, sir," she insisted, "The Miracle Tonic works. My Aunt Nettie used to walk with a cane, cause she had arthritis in her knee real bad. Now, she can waltz the night away!"

Papa replied, "Such witchery or 'hoodoo' is an abomination in the eyes of the Lord!" He said it quite loudly, in his church-testifyin' voice. So loud, that everyone in the small dining room all turned toward the Hurston clan, including the Professor.

Professor Zeke wore a huge, wicked smile, like the one he had on the posters, when he faced Papa. He announced, in his showman's baritone, "It seems like *someone* needs a nip of The Miracle Tonic, to calm their nerves!"

This pronouncement caused an eruption of laughter in the dining room. All of the Hurstons cringed, save Papa, who had the wrath of Moses throwing down the Golden Calf in him. Zora hated when he was like this; there was no talking to him. Mama tried; she placed her hand on his forearm and said, "John," in a soothing way. He just shook her hand off, like Zora knew he would.

"Charlatan," said Papa, "you should be ashamed of yourself. The only true healer is the Lord Jesus Christ!"

Professor Zeke looked positively relaxed. "Don't the Good Book say, He helps those who help themselves? Brother, I'm doing the Lord's work as well—just in a different way." The Professor's entourage clapped and added a few jeering *You tell 'em, Zekes* for good measure. In fact, most of the dining room clapped.

This made Papa truly angry. He stood up and threw down bills and coins on the table. "Come on, let's go. This place is clearly a nest of heathens." The rest of the Hurston clan followed him out of the restaurant. Zora stole a glance at Professor Zeke. He looked like a king in his court, and she couldn't help but feel a guilty twinge of awe at the power he commanded.

But Professor Zeke, like Hattie, was a fake, apparently.

"I should go," she whispered. Zora stood up, her eyes on the dirty floor of the shack. She heard Hattie sigh.

"Wait, child," Hattie said, and Zora watched as the conjure woman mixed some potion or other in a mason jar. It took maybe two minutes to complete. Hattie handed Zora a jar of liquid the color of pale amber. "This is peppermint tea with feverfew oil. It's good for headaches, even bad ones like your mama has. This might ease the pain."

"Thank you," Zora said. "I don't have much money—just a few pennies."

Hattie waved her hand, dismissing the question of payment. "Your mama getting well is payment enough."

"Thank you, Miss Hattie!" Zora put the mason jar on the table, and hugged the tall woman. Hattie seemed to be unused to being touched; she cautiously embraced Zora back.

Zora felt something tickle the back of her leg. "Oh!" she said, when she saw Teacake head-butt one of her legs. He purred loudly; it sounded like the motor of an old jalopy.

Hattie cracked a smile. "Child, Teacake likes you. And he don't like just anybody. He wants you to stay."

"I really must be getting back." Zora knew that Papa would ask a ton of questions about why she'd been so late coming home. Her mind was already constructing a bunch of stories.

"Well, let me read your future, at least."

Something dark stirred in her. Dark and—thrilling. Zora knew that fortune-casting was wrong, was something of the devil. Papa had pounded that into her skull. For some reason, it was way worse than asking for medicine from a witch. Fortune telling was a definite step away from Papa's teachings. It was defiant.

"Alright," Zora said, and something changed forever. She didn't know what, not yet. But this was the first step into—something.

Hattie cleared a space in the middle of her shack. The kerosene lamp light flickered, as did Teacake's eyes. The shadow fingers of herbs filigreed the lighted center. Hattie poured a burlap sack full of weirdly-shaped, ivory colored rocks on the ground in the cleared space. The pieces fell in a random shape. Hattie hunched over them, scrutinizing them carefully.

"Huh," she said.

Zora couldn't contain herself. "What do they say?"

Hattie looked up from the constellation. "Most unusual. The bones don't tell the usual story: love, marriage, children and death. No. Your path is different, child. There's love in there, yes. But mostly, you will be alone." Hattie pointed to a couple of odd shaped bones that might've been the legs of a dog. "But mostly, it's teeth and jawbones." She indicated a few ominous shapes in the far left of the loose circle. "You're a wanderer. Your path meanders, and leads you everywhere. The bones say, you're a storyteller of some kind. A keeper of secret lore and tradition." Hattie looked up into Zora's eyes, directly. It was an unsettling glance, full of wisdom and concern.

"The bones say that you're like me. Child, you are a conjure woman."

Death and Two Maidens

The Sad Fate of Prothenia Jenkins

Before she jumped into the Thames, Prothenia Jenkins thought she had reached the end. Everything would be erased. All the pain and shame. The waters churned, and gulls hovered above the brown and blue water. It hypnotized her. She waited. It was her last day on earth. So she watched as the sunset cooled into evening. Ruddy clouds took on violet and blue hues. She took in the smells, of excrement, piss, roasting chestnuts, the deep brine of the water. A last boat headed toward a dock. She glanced around. She was alone, truly alone. In the distance, a dog barked. Faces arose in her mind, her Papa and her sister Xenia, he in his favorite pork pie hat, she with each of her plaits ending in cornflower blue ribbons, the same color as her pinafore.

She jumped from the bridge.

She seemed to fall forever. Prothenia felt the wind stirring her hair, the cold seeping up under her small clothes. She remembered her sweet Maman and Grandmere. Soon, she would join them. Even the Creator would see that ending her life was best choice to be made, and perhaps, He would spare her soul from Gehanna. Down, down she went, like a stone. When she finally hit the water, it was like being stabbed by a cold knife. Instinctively, she struggled. But the bricks in the pocket of her heavy velvet cloak pulled her under. Her crinoline dress and undergarment soaked through, and the river dragged her down with dreadful efficiency.

She tried to breathe, and her lungs filled with the cold dark water. It was terrifying. She screamed, and the water rushed into mouth. It took her scream, her air, her life. As she sank, her vision faded. She died with her eyes wide open.

Life as the Ellworth's charwoman wasn't terrible. The work was endless—scrubbing flagstones and beating laundry, setting tables, cleaning night jars—basically, anything Mrs. Fromme, the head maid, refused to do. Mrs. Fromme was strict, a dour humorless woman with thin hair she kept confined in bonnet, her face the disagreeable color of boiled cabbage. But Prothenia had heard worse from other maids, of beatings and constant harassment. No, Fromme was fair, if cold.

Cook, on the other had, was positively wicked. She was a hag that could have been the descendant of one of the Macbeth witches. Indeed, she toiled over cauldrons that bubbled with unappetizing stews and ovens that produced burned roasts and breads. Her face was pocked and from her neck sprouted a goiter, the color of a pumpkin. For some reason, the Ellworths kept her on. Perhaps it was her imitation of a pious Christian woman when one of the Ellworths addressed her. To Prothenia, she was gruff and nasty.

It had been her second day on the job, and she sat at the kitchen table, attempting to eat the unburnt part of a roll when Cook turned on her.

"Dunno why they hired you."

Prothenia stayed silent, waiting. She could feel it in the air, Cook's cindery hatred. When Prothenia didn't respond, the hag continued, her back turned to her. "This is a respectable house."

"Am I not respectable enough to be a maid?" The words were out of her mouth before she could stop herself. (She could hear her Papa rebuking her: "Child, you have got to control that mouth of yours!")

"Not as far as I can see," Cook muttered.

"Not as far as you can see. What, pray tell, it is about me that you can see that makes me unfit? Perhaps, my skin, which is a few shades lighter than this nearly inedible roll you burned?"

Now, it was Cook's turn for silence.

"Listen, you. My grandmere was from the Caribbean. She was a grand conjure woman who consorted with, shall we say beings not of earthly make. She taught me a thing or two. Tricks. Spells. I suggest you not vex me too much, or who knows what might happen to dear, sweet Cook."

This elaborate lie had the intended effect. Cook stood still as statue. Did she shake? Prothenia was unsure, for just then Fromme swept in to the kitchen and began issuing orders in her brusque manner. Both underlings made haste to obey them. If Cook spoke to Fromme about her supposed witchery, she never knew. She suspected that Fromme would brush such accusations off as rubbish. Fromme didn't particularly care for Cook, and Cook was cowed by Fromme. Still, every now and then Cook would scowl at her, and she'd find cold tea or glue-like porridge left for her meals.

As for the Ellsworths themselves, they were a fine sort. The master was a barrister at some firm across town, for which he left at 6am and returned home at 7 in the evening. The missus was a fragile thing, always wrapped in shawls, even in high summer. She was also quite pregnant, due in a month or two. Life at the Ellsworth's, at least at that time, was slow and without drama. That all changed, when Trevor arrived.

A few months had passed. Mrs. Ellsworth gave birth to a girl, Phoebe; the child's care was yet another area of added responsibility. Not that Prothenia minded that much. Prothenia grew fond of the child and spent much time with her, as the child's mother rested. She sang her the songs that Maman used to sing to her. Even Cook called a silent truce against her, seeing how well Prothenia took to childminding. Not that they cared, but Prothenia had basically raised Xenia when Maman died and Papa worked his endless shifts. She wondered how the two of them were faring now.

One morning, as she was sipping milky tea, Fromme barged into the kitchen. She informed them that they were to have a guest, Mrs. E's brother Trevor. He'd come back for a long visit. He worked in India, importing various goods. Prothenia spent the rest of the day dusting, scrubbing, scouring various appliances. The good china—bone white with a decoration of blue willows and Chinese people, was to be used, and Cook was instructed to try not burn the evening meal. Prothenia spent the better part of the day preparing the guest room.

Trevor Whitford arrived in the early afternoon. Prothenia missed the excitement; she'd been told to tend to the nursery while Mrs. E welcomed him in the parlor. At six-thirty, Fromme took Phoebe from her.

"Go down and help that woman with the meal. I'm counting on you to make sure that it is at least, edible."

Dinner was served at seven-thirty. Prothenia entered the dining room bearing a tureen filled with a soup of boiled potatoes and beef. (When Cook was preoccupied with the dessert, Prothenia surreptitiously threw a handful of salt into the concoction, hoping it would impart some flavor). She almost dropped the dish when she entered the room where Mr. and Mrs. Ellsworth sat chatting with a strange young man.

For one thing, he was taller than either of them. He was a kind of giant. The plates in front of him were like children's toys. His hair—it was bright orange, with matching mutton chops and a pirate-like beard. He wore a kind of gold caftan, with buttons down the front shaped and colored like roses. There was no way he was not shocking.

In the second it took to regain her balance, Prothenia sussed out the room's dynamic. Mrs. Ellsworth was all titters and girlish sighs. She might have been in love with her brother. (They both shared watery green eyes as a feature). Mr E was visibly uncomfortable. He still wore his stiff work clothes, which had been starched stiff as boards. His face was pinched and he mostly looked at the tablecloth, as if escape might be found there among its pattern.

Fromme ladled out the soup with military efficiency as Prothenia followed her with the tureen. When they got to Mr Whitford, he said to his sister, "Lala, who is this beautiful Venus here?"

Mrs. Ellsworth said, "Mrs. Fromme?"

The red giant laughed. The sound was somewhere between a guffaw and a roar. (Mr. Ellsworth focused on his soup, attending to it as if it were the most delicious soup he'd ever had). "No. I meant the negress. La noire."

"Her? She's just the charwoman. Oh, Trevvie, tell me more about the Hindus. Is it true that they worship a god with the head of an elephant?"

"I will in a moment, Lala. What is your name?"

This, directed at her. Prothenia knew the rules of a household. Speak only when spoken to. Never meet your superior's eyes. But what was the rule when faced with such a peculiar situation? She chanced it, and told him her name, followed by a polite 'sir.'

"Prothenia. What a lovely name." He smiled at her, revealing some of the most disgusting teeth she'd ever seen. They were black and yellow, like the colors of a bee.

She was so shocked, she actually said—softly—"Oh my."

Prothenia felt relief that the rest of the evening she had to spend washing the dishes. It was chore that she hated, but there was something seriously unsettling about Mr. Whitford.

Prothenia gently knocked on the guest room door. She was full of— what? Dread?

"Do come in."

She turned the knob, then bent to pick up the breakfast tray that had a teapot and plate of black pudding and an acceptable slice of bread. She kept her eyes on the carpet as she bore the tray to Mr. Whitford's bedside.

"Thanks, love," he said. She curtsied, and turned to leave— He stopped her with a pawlike hand on her shoulder. "Not so fast, love."

This was too much. Prothenia felt her anger rising. It was one thing to be a maid; it was quite another to have one's private space invaded. She felt her tongue tingle with unspoken harsh words. Shrugging him off, she turned to face him.

"Listen, you—" she started. She stopped, stunned by the sight in front of her. Mr. Whitford was shirtless. He might have even been *nude*; his bottom half was covered by blankets. His skin was as pale as the belly of a fish. Over this was a thick layer of ginger fur. Two nipples, pink as pigs, poked out beneath the thicket. He smiled his ghastly smile.

"Prothenia, I have to pick up some some things from the city. My sister said that you would accompany me."

She had nothing to say to that.

"I should be ready by midday," he said, and began devouring his breakfast.

She'd never been to Limehouse Reach. She'd heard of it, of course, but she never had need to go there. Mr. Whitford seemed to have some business here. He seemed to know exactly where to go, in spite of his claims of ignorance. Prothenia was not surprised. He had the look of a liar about him. He fit right in, here. Men with busted faces, stinking of gin and fish, strolled along the river and its various taverns. These men all had the same horrible teeth that Whitford had—yellow teeth and black gums. Their eyes were rheumy or bloodshot. Ships that had seen better days listed in the dirty water; rough men scurried and scuttled around them like lice. No; she didn't like this area at all.

"Will we be long?" she asked him. He was absurdly dressed in suit that had fabric that shimmered. A top hat completed his look. "Cook said that she would like to get started on dinner soon, and I need to get some groceries..." (This was a lie). "We musn't tarry."

"That harridan can wait. I am sure time won't improve her questionable skills."

She didn't want to, but Prothenia laughed. A titter escaped, despite her best efforts.

"Now, there's a girl," he said. He wrapped his arm around her shoulder. They walked by the dock. Prothenia tried her best to ignore the stares of women in filthy bonnets and their beady-eyed children. Eyes that glittered bright with hatred. Look at him walking with his whore without the least bit of shame, those eyes said.

Presently, they turned down an alley cast in shadow. Pigeons cooed and fluttered away, disturbed by their arrival. One of them expelled a white globlet on the pavement. Prothenia did not like this place at all. She leaned against him instinctively. She felt that this was an evil place. The darkness and the silence all indicated this evil. It was a place where the sun never properly touched. Why had he bought her here? Prothenia felt that someone—or someones—were watching their every move.

Mr. Whitford let go of her, and approached a building. A single sign floated above a door that might have been painted red. She couldn't make out the words of the sign. Was it an image of a flower? The petals of the flower were curled, and sharp and weaponlike. And the writing— Prothenia knew her letters, but those strokes and curls made no English word. Mr. Whitford knocked on the possibly red door. After a moment, the door opened a sliver. She could see no-one in that slice, but she heard words directed at the ginger giant. Words that might have been English, but flavored with some other accent. After a brief exchange, the door opened wider. Mr. Whitford beckoned to her before he entered. Not knowing what else to do, Prothenia followed.

She was enveloped in a gloom of smoke and sweetness. She followed Mr. Whitford, who was following a small Chinaman. She'd only ever seen Chinamen from afar. This one wore a dark outfit with silver buttons down the middle. It was sort of like a priest's cassock. His head was bald and a long black plait sprouted from from his skull like some wild plant. The Chinaman led them to a sort of parlor with pillows on the floor instead more familiar settees and couches. The pillows were arranged in circles around something that looked like a monstrous tea-kettle. Men and a few women took puffs from nozzles that were connected to the tea-kettles, and emitted a floral grey smoke. Prothenia noticed that the windows of the building were covered with tapestries that depicted stylized bearded dragons and maidens in tight but ornately decorated robes. She watched the bubbling liquid in the belly of glass kettle. The faces of the silent smokers were blissful, if not outright asleep. Their faces drooped and drooled, and reminded her of the faces that Phoebe would make after she'd suckled at her mother's breast.

"Come, Prothenia," said Mr. Whitford. He followed the Chinaman to an unoccupied oasis of pillows. Dare she say no? She followed him reluctantly. She sat down, slightly away from him, and arranged her petticoats awkwardly. "I think you're in for a treat."

Papa would smoke the occasional cheroot. She found it distasteful. "Oh, no, Mr. Whitford. I do not smoke."

"I *insist*."

"Mrs. Ellsworth—your sister—she would not like me to smoke. Sir."

That ghastly, waspish smile spread across his face. "Lala need never know."

"But—"

"Hush. Just one puff, is all I ask."

During this exchange, a girl, also from China, set up the kettle with sleek efficiency, heating the water, sprinkling in the herbal mixture in one compartment. Water began to bubble, and smoke—more like mist—began to rise from one of the nozzles. Mr. W placed an ivory piece between his lips, and took a deep inhalation. He held it in his barrel-like chest, then let it go, slowly. Smoke came from his mouth and nostrils. He was like some kind of ginger dragon.

He shivered, then relaxed on the pillow. Heavily-lidded, he indicated that she should try. Prothenia knew that she shouldn't. The moans and drooling, the darkened room—all convinced that this was an evil place. But she had a shadow-self—a willful part of her that had long fallen from the arms of God. And it was this shadow-self that took the nozzle, and raised it to her lips.

She knew how to smoke from watching her father: by taking a long, slow breath. In went the mist, through her mouth. It coated her tongue with a taste of bitter earth and licorice. It rolled down her throat, gently numbing it, and down into her lungs. She held it in there—silver ephemeral gnats—then she let them rise and ooze out of her mouth, as if she were a black dragon. She coughed a bit. And felt nothing. What was the point?

Prothenia glanced at Mr. Whitford—"Trevvie." He sucked on the brass nozzle eagerly, swallowing smoke. All she felt was numbness and a slight dizziness. Prothenia took another puff. This time, the silver gnats were lazier. The flavor was intensified. It was truly horrible. Who would want to smoke such nasty stuff? Tobacco had a warm smell. This was like smoking an unsweetened tea brewed in castor oil.

And then—and then—

The smoke hit her brain. The silver gnats became silver balloons that rose and cooled her mind. She dropped the nozzle in her hand, and felt a warmth spread throughout her body. And it all made sense, every bit of it. Of course the room was dark; when you became a lantern, who needed outside light? Because she glowed. She knew that she did, a soft warm glow, tinged with lavender. She felt buoyant, a glowing jellyfish adrift on a dark sea. Her innards were brocaded with thin silver tissues...Prothenia did not hallucinate, not exactly. But dreamy images of increasing loveliness swirled around her, just the same. As the images faded—where she was a jellyfish, a lantern, a bird, a balloon—she took another puff of the marvelous magic smoke and they arose again.

How long she'd been in that reality, she couldn't say, but eventually, Mr. Whitford woke her, and led her from the dark room of smoke and dreams.

He recovered quite quickly, and became businesslike, almost as if they hadn't gone to a den of inequity. He said, when they were leaving Limehouse, "You said you had some provisions to pick up for Cook?"

Prothenia took a moment to answer. The cobblestones beneath her feet buckled and swayed. The sun looked like a rotten egg yolk in the blue and grey sky.

From far away, she heard him say, "Miss Jenkins?"

She opened her mouth to answer him. Something came out—maybe balloons or jellyfish or dragonsmoke—and hit the cobblestones with a disgusting splatter.

That was how it began. Initially she blamed Mr. Whitford, who only stayed for a week and did not accompany her again to that dark lounge. In fact, he practically denied it had every happened. She thought that the weird incident had been her imagination. Hadn't it? The waking dream beckoned her. She found herself longing for it during her work, which suddenly became tedious. Even her time with Phoebe. She dreamed about it at night. That jewel-like feeling—she'd never felt it before. Life had always been work, endless and forever. Down in Bristol, she'd helped her mother with sewing until her fingers bled. Then there was the washing up, cooking, taking care of her baby sister. Then, when Maman died, even more work. She left Bristol for more work in London, leaving behind her family. And for what? More endless toil. That time in the opium den was the first time she'd ever truly escaped the oppressive grind of her life.

Maybe two weeks had passed before Prothenia found herself down at Limehouse Reach again, searching for that hidden alley. She had the afternoon and evening off, and had coin. The bleak people gawped at her. She was used to it and besides didn't really care. She had a quest to fulfill. Into one alley and out of another she went, looking for sign of the flower. Some men pawed at her lewdly, said rude things. She said rude things back to them and searched on in the dying light, past alleys of drunks and dollymops. She wove through crowds of scallywags and the odd madwoman. Finally, she found it, unassumingly drenched in shadow.

Every free afternoon and evening was spent in the House of the Crimson Petals, imbibing dreams in her lungs. It didn't take long for the dragonsmoke to seep into every corner of her life, occluding and destroying it. Not that she cared. Prothenia was unsure whether she was let go from the Ellsworth residence or she just didn't bother to return. She had a vague recollection of harsh words with Mr. E, and Cook's triumphant grin. You could never be sure, when the world was a phantom. But somehow, she ended up sleeping in odd places. Boat holds, alleyways, strange men's—and sometimes—women's beds. Rookeries and residences. She floated through life, marking time until her next appointment in the land of silver haze.

That rudderless time ended abruptly one day. Prothenia went to the House of the Crimson Petals, only to find it abandoned. The door was slightly askew, so she pushed herself in. She saw a room filled with ripped pillows and smashed vases. The beds and mattresses were overturned, the tapestries were on the floor. Some dim instinct made her leave the place immediately. She left the alley, found another. She sat down, in her filthy, soiled clothing and cried.

"You."

She looked up to see a ruddy-faced woman with an unraveling bun. Her shawl was tattered, as were the edges of her petticoat. She leaned on a cane.

"You," she repeated with her cough of a voice, "get out of 'ere. I seen you before. You was always around that Chinamen's den. What's England come to, with all these slant-eyes and nignogs wanderin about. Anyways, it's all over. The coppers came and cleaned that place out. If I see the likes of you round here again, I'll let the coppers know, and they'll put you in prison. Now get!"

The old Prothenia would have given the crone a mouthful. But this new one, filled with endless need and despair just left the alley and Limestone Reach.

She wandered around for a day, maybe more. Faces and memories arose, unsummoned—Maman, her father, Xenia. She'd let them all down. She hated what she'd become. She was a ghost, and wispy and insubstantial as smoke. She'd been destroyed.

She found herself at the ledge of a bridge.

In which Prothenia rises, and her subsequent adventures

Mist rose from the river in the early morning, and Prothenia rose with it. At first, she couldn't separate herself from the mist. She had no shape. It was vaguely disconcerting, but she allowed herself to drift down the river with the mist, until the sun burned it away. Then she was alone. She hovered above the filthy Thames like a moth. She tried to look at her hands, but they were invisible. As was the rest of her.

What am I, she asked herself. It was patently clear that she was some kind of ghost. She had heard of such things; once she and her sister Xenia had played with a YesYes board, much to the consternation of Papa. But she never put much stock or belief in the supernatural, beyond a noncommittal acknowledgment of the Lord during holiday times. When she'd jumped last night she hadn't given it a thought. She had just wanted to escape the horror her life had become. Going to Heaven and being reunited with Maman or, conversely, being tossed like a rag into the darkest corner of Hell never really entered her mind. She supposed she was in some kind of limbo, until Jehovah decided what to do with her.

Right now, she couldn't just hover above the water. Perhaps she could leave it. Oddly enough, though she had no body and couldn't see herself, even as a transparent specter like the ghosts in those penny dreadful novels, she could smell. In fact, her sense of smell was even better. It was more intense. She smelled mud, fish, rot, damp, and offal. She could only imagine what created such a heady stew—

The thought became an action, and she was beneath the waves. On the bottom of the river, things slithered and and oscillated in the slow churn of the deep. She saw the skeleton of an infant—laudanum dreams and tiny pale bones, a heart like a small orange. The ghost of a cat prowled around, leaping at a diseased fish. A small ship lay wrecked, the wood warped and devoured by algae. She heard the sounds of the world above, distorted and stretched beneath the waves. A clanging bell—

She was high above the city in a church tower, the sound sent ripples, sounds the color of the bell she was next to. Pale gold sounds, with a film of dinge. The boy who rang the bell was gangly and awkward. Fish-belly white skin, lips the shade of liver, and bright orange hair. Hair that reminded of Mr. Whitford—

And she found herself in the Ellsworth's house. She was in her room—her old room. She recognized it immediately: the small bed, the scraped wardrobe, the stone floor. It was empty—of course it would be. What reason did they have to keep her meager possessions? It was dark and closed up. The lone window was covered by a heavy drape. How she had hated that room. And yet, it had been home. Prothenia felt a tinge of sadness. It spread throughout her—body? *Body*. She didn't have a body anymore. She was nothing.

I couldn't even manage a proper death.

Before she plunged completely into despair, the door to the room suddenly opened. In walked Mrs. Ellsworth, carrying Phoebe.

"...what happened to her. One day, she wasn't around. I do hope she didn't meet some misadventure. You're always hearing about horrible things happening out in the street. Well. This is it."

Behind Mrs. Ellsworth, a young woman walked. She was a shade darker than her own hue—(when she had a hue). She was tall and slightly plump. Her hair hadn't been tamed—it was bushy and full, unconfined by hairpins or relaxers. She had a thick posterior and her blouse was filled with her ample bosom.

"What are the wages, ma'am?" she asked. Her voice was beautiful—it had a silvery tone—and it was scented with an Islands accent.

Mrs. E named a price that was slightly below what Prothenia had been paid.

"Those wages are acceptable," said the woman. "I can start immediately, if you like."

Mrs. E seemed to relax. "I will let your supervisor, Mrs.. Fromme, know. She will provide you with your uniform and assign your duties. But please, feel free to settle in...what did you say your name was?"

"Felicity Smyth."

"Felicity, yes. Please excuse me. I have to put Phoebe down for a nap." Mrs. E retreated.

Prothenia observed the plump girl unpack a modestly sized valise. A second dress, small clothes, stockings...and a doll. But the word doll was inadequate. Its heartshaped face was molasses-dark, with shining pearl buttons for eyes. Its hair was a wisp of white feathers, many of them intricately braided together, to form strands. It wore a satin gown of a lurid pink color, a shade that hurt eyes. What was more, it stank. A musky scent, like animal fetor, underneath a floral, syrupy scent. Prothenia looked at it closely.

She became aware of how amorphous she was. She was a shimmer of memories and feelings. The doll mesmerized her. She felt herself being drawn to it. It was breathing her in...and Prothenia wanted to be drawn in. She was devoured by the musky-sweetness, the cruel pink. She could rest in bed of satin, flowers and feathers forever...

The spell was abruptly broken when Felicity put the doll on the wardrobe shelf, and closed it.

Three clipped knocks stalled Felicity's unpacking. In marched Fromme, with her sour lemon expression. "Mrs.. Ellsworth tells me that you are to join our household..."

Prothenia untethered herself from the room.

Mr. Saturday makes an unwelcome appearance

There was whiteness, an endless expanse. Clouds, milk, smoke—she roiled through it, became a part of it. Prothenia did not think, did not remember. It was like her time at the House of the Crimson Petals, sailing through a gentle haze of oblivion. Whenever a thought or image arose—Maman singing one of the songs from the islands, her sister Xenia laughing at some joke they'd shared—Prothenia submerged herself in the whiteness. The oblivion rushed over her formlessness. This was death. Death was white and dreamless. If she wasn't in heaven, she certainly wasn't in hell either.

She settled in the silt, and let the waters of oblivion smooth her away.

There came a time—a day, an hour—that the milk curdled. The whiteness was stained and gently disturbed. It started as a current, a tugging at her essence. If Prothenia were a stone at the bottom of a river, she became dislodged. Whatever shell she lived in shattered like glass. And she became amorphous once more. Memories flooded her. The dreamless time was over.

An image of her sister came to her. Maybe I can see her once more, she thought. Whatever etheric process that let her travel—or haunt— began. A fading of her glimmering—

It stopped, violently. Prothenia had thought she was beyond pain. She was wrong. She was ripped from the oblivion like a rag from a clothing line. Plucked, like a rose from the vine. Breath—how long it had been since she could breathe?—flowed from her, as if she'd been punched in the ribs. Ribs—did she have them now? She couldn't focus on the miracle of having a body again, though. Her pain swept through her, from her scalp to her toes.

-No.

The word was not spoken. It echoed in the chamber of her skull.

-You thought you escaped my notice, child.

The voice traveled up her spine, in tectonic vibrations. She glanced up from the marshy ground that her newly restored form knelt on. The medicinal sweet smell of rum hit her full in the face. It made her nauseous.

What she looked into froze whatever feeling she had.

The *thing* standing before her wore a suit of liquid black. The white ruff of a shirt peeked up behind the V a buttoned jacket made. A matching stovepipe hat rose up on its head. But the head— It had no skin. None, at all. Yellow bone, fractured here and there, where cheeks and a nose should be. It stared at her with rotten eyes the color of worms. These eyes were rimmed with scraps of old muscle, now the color of diseased meat. The blackened teeth, uncontained by lips, grinned at her horribly. Its face was yellow and black, the colors of a bee. The grin reminded her of Mr. Whitford.

It was this association that broke the trance of horror. Prothenia filled with something hot. The hot feeling rose to her brain, and made her stand. Mr Whitford—surely a *human* demon of some kind—had ruined her life. She would not let him ruin her death.

Every vile thing she'd heard on the streets of London came to her lips. She cursed the thing loudly. The dragonsmoke she'd inhaled became dragonfire. The demon took the invective silently. When she had finished, it responded calmly.

-You are high-spirited, indeed, child. Still, come with me you must.

He placed his hand on her hers. His hand was covered with skin, but it was corpse skin. Papery and fissured. Prothenia found the contact revolting. The skin slithered over hers.

"Sir, where are you taking me?"

-Where you belong.

That strange rage rose up in her again. Prothenia shook loose from his grip, and lost her shape. She slipped into—

"She's a hard enough worker, she is," Cook was saying to Fromme over a cup of tea. It was late afternoon in the Ellsworth kitchen. As always, something was bubbling in a stew pot. "But she's strange."

"How so," Mrs. Fromme asked. She wasn't looking at Cook; she was probably inspecting the cleanliness of the kitchen stealthily.

"I hear her, singing some beastly music. And smell the most awful smoke coming from her room. It's spicy. Mr. Whitford burnt a couple of them sticks. What did he call 'em—*incest*?"

"Incense," Fromme corrected without cracking a smile.

"Yes. I know the good book says not to judge, but she gives me the willies. She don't smile. And she looks like that *Hottentot Venice* woman. What if she worships them islands' gods? I hear they kill goats and offer them blood."

Fromme gulped the last of her tea. "You've been reading too many of those lurid novels, in my humble opinion." She placed the cup on the counter and left the room in a sweep of dark skirts." Prothenia listened to this exchange as she regained her bearings. Why—how—had she gotten here? Something had pulled her here. Maybe it was her connection to the room. Then why not the abandoned House of Crimson Petals, or, indeed, her family in Bristol? Then she remembered Felicity and her doll. Something sparked in her. Grandmere was a Christian, but she had been raised on Saint Lucia. She'd spoken of a religion there, one with spirits and dark arts. Beings that controlled the roads between life and death. She'd somehow gotten one of those spirit's attention. The pink robed doll in Felicity's suitcase she'd seen briefly before she fled to the dreamless place had been soaked in some puissant power. The doll's pull had been strong, but not necessarily evil.

Prothenia did not have a plan, not really, as she shimmered away from the kitchen and glimmered into her old room. Almost at once, she felt the presence of whatever lived in the doll. It called to her, in a voice that smelled like roses and treacle. It was a pink sound, as delicate as the tongue of a kitten. It called to her from the wardrobe door. Not knowing what else to do, Prothenia drifted towards it. Through the wood and into the bosom of the feathered and soft spirit. It welcomed her with a lazy warmth.

Prothenia emerged from the clutches of the soft spirit. It was like waking up from a long sleep. She remembered, faintly, whispering and singing. Grandmere knew a little French from Saint Lucia, mostly in the form of songs. (Grandmere was born a French citizen; she'd died a British subject. The two languages mingled.) These songs reminded Prothenia of those songs, whose words she didn't quite remember. How long she'd been hidden in the doll, she couldn't tell. She opened her eyes—she had a shape once more—in the middle of her old room.

The girl who'd replaced her, Felicity, knelt in front of the little pink goddess. The doors to the wardrobe were open. Two candles flanked the doll, embroidering it with shadow. Felicity looked as if she were in a trance. She said a prayer with her marvelous silvery voice, honoring the doll, which she called *Erzulie Freda*. Prothenia felt as if she were eavesdropping. But she couldn't risk leaving the room. The demon man lurked out there, in the world.

It doesn't matter anyway. I am dead, and she can't see me, Prothenia thought.

"I can hear you just fine."

Prothenia started. Felicity continued, "But I can't see you. Freda can, though. She can't give me the gift of spirit-sight—not yet, anyway." Felicity turned and gazed in the general direction of where she was. She smiled. She had the whitest teeth Prothenia had ever seen.

"Why don't you tell me who you are?"

Prothenia opened her mouth. No sound came out. She hadn't spoken before, and yet this girl had heard her.

She impelled thought toward Felicity: *I am Prothenia Jenkins. I used to work here.*

Felicity sat on the bed after blowing out the candles. She was in a nightgown, illuminated by the lone lantern that the Ellsworth's provided her with. Prothenia remembered that lantern. It cast out weak light. Now, it was the brightest thing in the whole world. She'd been lonely for months, maybe a year since she'd moved to London.

"Tell me about yourself, Miss Jenkins," Felicity said in the pause.

Prothenia spoke more than she had in all that time. She told Felicity about her family in Bristol, Papa in his pork pie hat, Xenia's mischievous pranks. Her Maman's death, Grandmere's stories. Yes, she told the story of her demise (leaving out certain unseemly bits), but mostly, she was happy to talk to someone. Felicity's story was similar, though her family lived in London. She'd looked for work when her aunt came from Antigua. There simply wasn't enough room in their flat.

When Prothenia got to the part about the man in the top hat, Felicity sat up. (She had long since blown out the lamp).

"Baron Samedi," Felicity said. "Mr. Saturday. I am quite familiar with him. I have never met him, of course. But my father had encountered him once, when he was a boy. He is a wicked man, but like all of the *loa*, he can be bargained with. You should not worry, though. You are under Erzulie's protection."

Thank you, Prothenia said. She would have hugged Felicity, if she could have.

"Thank me?" Felicity laughed. "You should thank Erzulie. She is the one who called you. She is the one who blessed you, and made you her daughter."

A month passed. Two or more. Time had no real meaning for her anymore. Prothenia spent much of her existence with Erzulie Freda, her world of flowers and jewels and dreams. That time was inchoate, indescribable. It was about singing perfume, or dancing colors, or tasting dreams. The world whirled by on song and myth. When Prothenia emerged from her time in that wonderful place, she would find a week or more had passed.

Felicity, when she was around, would fill her in about the world of the living. Phoebe could walk now. Mrs. Ellsworth had a cough that wouldn't leave her, and she refused a tincture that Felicity had made. Cook and Fromme were ever the same. For her part, Prothenia tried to explain what the spirit world was like. She didn't have the language. It was as good an existence as she'd ever had.

One evening, when she'd emerged from the jeweled plane, Felicity sat up immediately. The girl still couldn't see her, but she was getting better at sensing her presence.

"Prothenia," said Felicity. "You are here." There was something odd about her tone.

You sound disappointed.

Felicity laughed. "I assure you I am not. It's just...."

How long have I been gone?

"A few weeks. I have news. Mr. Whitford is here again."

Prothenia did not know what to say. Or feel. She said nothing. She was half-surprised to find that he was alive.

Felicity went on: "Mrs. Ellsworth has taken a turn for the worse, I'm afraid. In that time, Mr. Ellsworth contacted the missus' family...."

Beware of him, Felicity. Do not be alone with him!

"There is no need to worry, sister. He is quite in a state. I suspect that his addiction to opium has gotten rather worse."

Poor Phoebe! Mrs. Ellsworth and I were never really friendly, but I do not wish ill on her....

Her thought was interrupted by the most blood-curdling howl. Something smashed in the kitchen directly above the room.

"What on earth?" Felicity sat up. It was night; she grabbed the lantern and headed toward the door. Prothenia intended to follow her, but found that she could not move. It felt as if she were weighted down or glued to the floor. She tried to warn Felicity, but her thoughts had turned to mud, like the sludge that was in the bottom of the Thames, where her body lay.

The door smashed open, and in the frame stood Mr. Whitford. Time and opium had not been kind to him. He was thin, and the fire of his hair had dulled. The skin around his face was stretched taut. His face was a skull.

"There you are, my sweet dark Negress." His voice was nasal and cracked.

"Mr. Whitford?" Felicity began meekly.

He pushed her away, smashing her head against the wall. Mr. Whitford stared at the space where she was stuck. His watery green eyes darkened to the color of worms. He smiled his ghastly smile. Bone yellow teeth, black gums. He licked his teeth with a black tongue. Prothenia smelled rum on him.

"Thought you could escape me, did you?" Prothenia knew that horrible, bone-rattle of voice. Mr. Saturday was in there, festering in Trevor Whitford's soul. Nausea filled her. "No-one escapes me." And Mr. Saturday stepped from Whitford's ruined flesh. It was an awful, psychic sound—the rending of souls. Whitford collapsed next to Felicity, who was bleeding from her temple.

-The game is over.

He reached and grabbed her arm with his disgusting skin. Prothenia was frozen, without agency. Mr. Saturday dragged her essence across the floor. The door to her room had become some kind of portal. Marsh-mist and the scent of rum oozed through the portal.

"Stop, you old fool."

Baron Samedi stopped in his tracks. Felicity stood up. She was still bleeding, but Prothenia knew that it wasn't just Felicity. Some other being rode her flesh. Sweetness stained the air, and Felicity's eyes sparkled like agates.

"She is mine," Felicity said in her silvery voice. "My daughter."

-Woman, he rumbled, you dare to challenge me?

"I dare," she replied.

When the goddess stepped from Felicity's body, the effect was gentler. It was like the parting of curtains. What emerged was a being that was flower, fabric, and woman. She was spun in soft rose petals that covered most of body. Jewels dripped from her ears, on her fingers in rings. Samedi scowled and lunged at Erzulie. She gracefully evaded him, and grew like a flower into room. With both hands, she separated Samedi from Prothenia.

-This is my sacred space. You have the world. Go, and wander.

Samedi struggled in her grasp. He was like a little boy having a tantrum. Like a patient mother, Erzulie restrained him. Both of them faded from the air.

A homecoming, of sorts

The candles flickered and shadows danced over the face of Erzulie. Both girls, one living and one dead, paid her tribute.

Afterwards, Felicity lay in bed. She could see Prothenia clearly now.

She broke the silence: "Mrs. Ellsworth went to see her brother. I overheard her talking to Mr. Ellsworth at dinner. Seems he's doing much better. He no longer speaks of skull-faced demons."

Prothenia let some moments pass before she asked, Do you think Samedi will ever bother me again?

Felicity sighed. "Prothenia, I've told you. We're Her daughters. And even if he does dare to 'bother' you again, I'll protect you."

It was moments like these that she wished she could hold Felicity's hands.

Sugardaddy

August 15

I hate it here. Mama say, Just give it a chance Tasha. But I can't. I hate it.

Mercury Towers is ugly as sin. Sixteen stories of brick the color of old blood that have these roach-infested tiny apartments and hallways with concrete floors, caged lights and broken elevators. I think the apartment in *Good Times* was better. At least I can see the Monument from my window. It's so white, against the dirty sky and the even dirtier river.

Because the walls are concrete we can't hear our neighbors fighting and fucking, but in the halls you can smell cooking cabbage and Clorox. And there's always gangsta rap and whatever *cucaracha* shit those Latinos play blaring through the halls.

New beginnings, Mama says.

Fuck new beginnings.

August 18

I was down in the laundry room when I saw this strange looking crackhead nigga out of the corner of my eye.

The laundry room is bright yellow, like a pimp's hat, with brown floors that have gum so old that it's black. It's near the loading dock and there's this one apartment nearby with a scratched up door. Half the machines have OUT OF ORDER signs on them, and it smells like dirty socks. At least it's cool, not like that swampy air that clings to your skin outside. (Another reason why I hate it here). After another lady finished folding her clothes, I was the only one left in the room. Only the swishing washing machine and the rumbling dryer were my company. I turned on my iPod and listened to Usher.

I noticed the smell first. It tickled the back of my throat with its sweetness. It was a familiar smell, one that bought me back to summers at Granddad's farm where the grass grew until it had a little hat of seeds on top of each stalk; where birds and flies sizzled in the air; where a thousand cicadas and crickets fought like competing boomboxes. It smelled like grape soda, not that natural shit that mixes grape juice and sparkling water. It was sweet as teeth rot and tasted *purple*. This smell filled my nostrils, like pollen. I turned around, expecting to see someone with a plastic bottle. What I saw was this:

A thin man, with skin so dark it was purple. What little hair he had was white. He was shirtless, but I couldn't see any nipples on him, and he wore reddish brown corduroys that had an extension cord as a belt. *His eyes were white*, like dead things.

I was jamming to Usher—

I dropped my iPod—

And screamed.

He ran, taking his fake grape soda smell with him.

August 22

This girl, Shanté, she lives on our floor. She's darker than me, a little bigger than me, and is always eating Funyuns. She saw me once in the lobby and we rode the broke-ass elevator up together, and she asked me what I had on my iPod. Turns out she got an iPod from her dad, a mini, but she didn't have no computer so she couldn't put any music on it.

Dad's stupid like that, she said.

I smiled but didn't say nothing. I was thinking about my own dad, and how I'd do anything to have a *stupid* dad.

So I invited her back to my room so she could load up some songs from my laptop.

She's my age, a couple of months more, and it turns out that she goes to the school I'm transferring to. We talked about teachers and classmates to watch out for. She also told me about Mercury Towers and gave me the 411. Who sold what, who to avoid, who was in MS13. She told me all this, spraying yellow crumbs of Funyuns everywhere. She's nice, but kinda gross.

I asked her about that weird dark guy I'd seen in the basement a couple of days ago.

She looked at me like I'm tripping or something, and said, Naw, I ain't *never* seen a half nekkid nigga like that.

He was there, I said, in the laundry room, all crazy looking. I screamed.

Shanté laughed. There's lots of niggas on rock—and even PCP. I ain't surprised at all. They look like they jumped outta they bodies. He must be *new*.

August 25

Shit! My hand is still shaking, But I gotta get this down *now*.

Before Mama went to her job at the hospital, she asked me—told me—to do some of her laundry since she didn't want me laying around and watching *Maury* and judge shows all day. I must've rolled my eyes at her cause she said, Girl, don't you start with me. Honestly I didn't mind. I figured I'd do the laundry in the morning and then ask Shanté if she wanted to go to the Mall after; maybe she could show me around. (I still ain't seen the sights; since I'm here I might as well enjoy it, right?) So I grabbed the basket of dirty scrubs—most of 'em printed with silly lollipops and smiling bears—and went to the basement. It was still morning, and I did not bring my iPod this time. I did not want to be surprised if that weird nigga showed up again. Instead I bought a book, one of Mama's, called NATURE OF A SISTA that showed some skinny heffa in a red dress with a gun.

Thank Jesus I was not alone, I thought as I entered the laundry room. A friendly woman, named Tammie, who's light-skinned, was hogging all of the working washing machines. When she saw me, she said, I'm almost done with one of 'em, honey. A couple of minutes later she moved one load into a free dryer. She sat down to watch the little hand-held TV she had (I gotta watch my stories, she said). I started reading the book. There was a rape on page one and a drug deal gone bad on page eight—it was real good. I only looked up when I smelled it again. That purple chemical smell.

I must've looked all weird cause Tammie saw me and said, What's wrong, sweetie?

She'd gotten a grape soda out of the machine and was sipping it.

Nothing, I said, and went back to the book. But I couldn't concentrate anymore. The smell, sugary, fake, and the sound of the tiny voices coming from her tiny TV knocked me out of the book. Instead, I scanned the pages of NATURE OF A SISTA and listened to the whir and buzz of the machines around me.

When I looked up from the blurry page, I saw him standing in the doorway.

His darkness. His noseless face. His mouth, disjointed, toothless. His eyes, white and pupiless. He stood in the door for a moment, the two slits where his nose would have been taking in the air of the laundry room. Detergent, damp, and dust. He moved then towards Tammie, and, I knew, the grape soda smell. To say he walked would be wrong. He—flickered. Like those clubs that have strobe lights and you disappear for a moment in a flash and you found that your arm has moved again. Like you're in a black and white film. But the flicker-walking was more intense when he did it. In and out of sight, like he faded completely from the world. He crept toward Tammie, who was still looking at her story on the small black and white TV. In and out, off and on, each step appearing like it was sent on a bad TV station. Tammie didn't notice him. I musta made a noise or something cause she looked up at me with You OK written on her face. But I was frozen—my voice stuck in my throat when I realized that she couldn't see the freaky ghost nigga creeping up on her.

The nigga walked right behind Tammie. She was focused on her story. He did some weird juju with his hands—that had long gross finger nails—over her head. A cloud of something like gnats except smaller rose from her head and shoulders. They were different colors, like Skittles or M&Ms. He opened his horrible mouth, with teeth like glass, and ate the tiny cloud of candies. I heard the crunch. The smell of sugar burst on the air, in all its forms. Soda, burnt caramel, cotton candy. Large crunchy crystals on muffin tops, powdered on donuts, or dissolved in sweet tea. My tongue watered for it.

I also felt sick. The expression on his zombie face was terrible. And the expression on Tammie's face... Her eyes were half-closed like she was drowsing. A smile played at the corner of her lips. But I couldn't look away.

When he finished sucking the cloud down, he looked right at me. He licked his tongue at me, and slunk out of the laundry room. Tammie opened her eyes, and resumed watching her stories like nothing had happened.

September 3

School sucked. I knew it would. First, it was hot. There was no air conditioning in the whole building, which meant it was like 200 degrees inside. Second, no-one was friendly. I knew they wouldn't be; I told Mama that but she ignored me, telling me that I would make new friends soon enough. When they did acknowledge me, they acted like I was Bama. Third, the one girl I did know, Shanté, didn't share any of my classes, on account of her having to repeat her grade. I saw her at lunch, briefly, but she was with a group of her friends and I didn't feel like introducing myself. I ended up alone, hating my situation.

I guess I should try to be more positive. That, and face facts. Mama left Daddy cause he was fucked up. And he was outta control. Always sweating, and skinny, like he was sweating out his flesh.

I remember the night when he looked like he hated me. Stop texting on that phone about me, he screamed at me.

I'm not, I told him.

You a liar, he said.

Daddy, I said.

And he said, *Don't call me that.*

Then he snatched the phone outta my hand and threw it against the wall. It shattered. All the beads and crystals I glued on it scattered across the floor.

September 6

Hell. Yesterday was hell.

1. One of the boys in my class started in on me. In between class, in the hallway, he called me 'Squasha.' Ha ha. Very funny. By lunchtime, it had turned into Sasquatch. The boy, Kenyatta, had a group of his friends around him. He was pretending to be one of those ghost hunter types you see on TV, all like, *Let's watch it in its native habitat.*

Quit playing with me, I said.

It appears to be irritated, he told his crowd. They snickered like a bunch of retards.

I know I am a big girl. But I ain't no damn Bigfoot!

I was sitting alone by the cafeteria window. I was almost done anyway. I stood up and went to bus my tray.

Someone in his crew said *Badonkadonk.*

Giggle hiss hahahaha.

Stop it, I said. Louder this time.

Kenyatta: *It roared!*

By this time most of the cafeteria was watching us. They all sat, silent as dolls. They were watching the drama, like we were on Jerry Springer. Why didn't anyone help me? Drama must taste sweet.

Well, if they wanted drama, I'd give it them.

I threw my dessert, vanilla pudding, at him. It fell short, but some of it splattered on his sneakers.

Ooo, some girl said. Laughter.

Don't fuck with me, I said.

But Kenyatta didn't give a shit. He said, *Observe. It flings its feces like a gorilla at the zoo.*

His audience—the whole cafeteria—fell out like they were on *Def Comedy Jam.*

I went to the bathroom and washed my face several times. The water helps hide the tears.

2. Mom woke up screaming at 5:30 yesterday morning. I sat straight up.

Mom, what's wrong, I said.

Fuck, she said, along with a bunch of other curse words.

I knew it was serious, whatever it was. I went to her room and saw her standing up. Her arms were outstretched and she was examining them. They were covered by a rash that was red even under her dark brown skin.

I asked what that was. She didn't know, and started scratching herself and said it was damn poison ivy. I began to itch, too, and we both found that I had the same rash. The itch was different than a regular itch. It *tingled*, and no amount of scratching satisfied it. It felt like my *bones* were itching. Mom told me to stop scratching—even as she was scratching. We'd have to get some Calamine lotion at the drug store today. We had no idea what it was.

There was a part of me that immediately thought of the monster in the laundry room. Maybe it spread poison... But there was no way I was gonna tell anyone about him. Other people couldn't see him, apparently, so they would think I was whack.

Back in my room, I saw something, the size of an appleseed, scuttle across my sheets. I opened up the blinds, flooded my room with light. The Monument was against the orange soda sun, like a syringe. The smell hit me at once. Metallic, tangy and spicy. And it was coming from my bed. First, I stripped it. Nothing was there. So I followed the awful smell and flipped up the mattress.

It was sheer horror there, as bad as seeing that invisible crack man. Tiny bugs the color of old dried shit scurried and scuttled on the boxpsring. There were splotches of black on the ripped cover of the boxspring that looked like a damned oil spill. I saw two of them squiggling—they were fucking! One was on top of another one, and had his sharp ass stabbed into the other bug's guts. I shuddered as one of the bugs crawled up my arm. I dropped my mattress and crushed the thing. It exploded, like a bomb made of blood.

I was tripping this time. I was going, *Mom, Mom!*

She was in the doorway, *What is it, baby?*

I pointed to the mattress; where it fell you could see the squiggling crawling creepy fucking crazy bugs and their black shit.

Both of us looked at them like we were characters in a Wes Craven movie.

This building sucks!

3. I called up Nana. When it gets too much, she's the one I can talk to. It's always been that way. I guess that she's my best friend. I told her about it all—except the grape soda-colored man. School, bed bugs, etc. I even cried.

When I finished she said, *Your daddy called me last night. He's looking for y'all.*

I didn't say nothing.

I didn't know what to feel. Was he looking for us because he was better? I hoped that was so. I got excited.

But she burst my bubble, almost like she could read my mind. *He ain't doing too good. He cussed at me and said he would hurt me if I didn't tell him where y'all was. I told him I didn't know and hung up. Didn't answer the phone after that.*

She paused. And in that pause, I saw Daddy, or what he'd become. I saw the soda machine he'd punched one time when it ate his dollar bill. The shattered glass, his bloody fist. And him not blinking or even noticing when blood dripped down his arm.

I didn't tell Mom about the phone call with Nana. Daddy's on the other side of the country. She doesn't have to worry about him.

September 9

School let out early today—teachers' conferences—and Mom wouldn't be home for hours. I didn't give a shit about the stuff on TV. So I was bored. I thought about calling Nana but I didn't really have anything new to say to her. Besides, I was avoiding something.

I had to know.

This time, I didn't have any laundry to do. The building was empty, or so it seemed as I rode down the elevator to the basement. I studied the graffiti knifed into the wood grain. *Donetta loves Trevaughan.* Some shit in Spanish. I noticed how dirty it was. The light panel had a billion dead bugs in it. No wonder we had bed bugs. When the door opened, I stepped into the silent hallway. I was relieved to hear some of the washing machines going, but the laundry room itself was empty. Someone had taken up three machines. I saw the white foam swirling around and around. It made no sense for me to be down here to just watch machines spinning, like a damned dog. I went to the soda machine and got a grape soda without thinking about it. When I opened it, I smelled *him*. And I knew that I'd done the right—or the wrong—thing. As I sipped it, I read the label. High fructose corn syrup hit my tongue along with the carbonated water. I burped after the first gulp. There was tartaric acid. I guess that was the grape flavor. And Red 40, Blue 1, colors made in some tricked-out laboratory by a scientist with crazy hair.

You know in cartoons, when something smells good, they have these wavery almost invisible lines that draw a character to an apple pie sitting on a window ledge? It must have been like that with him. What words can I use to show how off the hook his walk was? It was almost balletic—I swear he was walking on his tippy-toes. But I couldn't be sure cause his feet were all fucked up—twisted, scaly skin, too few toes on one foot, too many on the other. Same thing with his hands and fingers. He didn't seem to be bothered by it. His eyes were closed, as if in pleasure, and he was smiling.

He almost came right up to me, and opened his eyes. They were white, like milk. Or crack cocaine. He skin was dark purple. I ain't never seen a purple nigga before. Blue-black, yes. But not *purple*. What little hair he had on his skull was blond but kinky. He was shirtless and still wearing those nasty corduroys. Did he have any other clothes? He smiled at me. The glass teeth reflected the piss poor laundry room light. He was one ugly motherfucker. But with his almost purple skin and glass teeth, he was also kinda pretty. I mean, L'il Wayne is both ugly and pretty like that—the wild mess of his prison tattoos and fugly grill distracts you from his hot body and pretty baby face. I was scared—who wouldn't be? But at the same time, I knew that he wouldn't hurt me. I don't know why. Maybe because he knew I was the only one who could really see him.

I offered him the soda.

He ignored it, and did a balletic gesture with his clawed hands, telling me to follow him. (His long nails were frosted glass).

I did the stupid thing that white girls in horror movies always do. I followed him. Looking back, I should have been more careful, but I don't know. I just *had* to follow him. Maybe that was his magic, or whatever. I couldn't keep my eyes off of him. He shifted in and out, blurred, and skipped. There are certain sound effects in hip hop records. Scratches, hisses, swells. They would be the perfect soundtrack to the way he walked.

Down one hall we went, then another, where the overhead lights were off. He stopped in front of a door, rust red and scratched, which he opened. I followed him in. Maybe I wanted to die. There ain't a lot to live for. Maybe Mom and Nana. But that was all. My family was ruined. I hated the new school and wasn't too crazy about the city. I had no friends. I was 300 pounds, if I bothered to admit it. Who wants to fuck that, except some perv? I would probably die early anyway. So I guess it was a death wish.

The room was a mess. That didn't surprise me. There was a mattress on the floor, stained, with just loose sheets on the cover. The ceiling had the crisscrossing pipes stretched across a concrete backdrop. There were piles of things, neatly arranged here and there. Old brown-amber prescription bottles, some of them still with pills. There was a mountain of gleaming syringes. One wall had candy wrappers glued to it, with names of candy bars I'd never even heard of, some of them in different languages. Perfume bottles marched along a floor, before they changed into weird alcohol bottles. It was junk, but it was neatly arranged. Another thing: it smelled sweet in here—a smell that I recognized but couldn't recall the name of. The white-eyed nigga was smiling at me. He was obviously proud of his little crib.

What do you want? I said. If I was gonna die, I wanted it over with quickly. No endless reveals of horrible things.

He came toward me, the glass teeth glittering like a tricked out grill.

I braced myself for the bite.

Instead, I got a kiss.

His lips were cool, like peppermint. His breath went into me, and my lungs. I might have felt the flicker of his tongue; I wasn't too sure. And it was over soon, cause I pushed him away.

I cussed at him, *Freak*. I got ready to run, but something stopped me. It hit me all at once. Taste and smell. It was all one thing. And the world became…delicious! How can I describe it? Take the pipes that ran the length of the room. I could *taste* them. The cool condensation on the pipes, the scaly red rust, the iron, the algae, the mold…I know it sounds gross, but I felt that I could eat the whole effing ceiling. I looked at the mountain of syringes, and I could smell what had been in them. The visions blew my mind. I saw blood, yes, but also chemicals. I don't have names for them. But the flavors—they were beyond Baskin Robbins' 31! How do you taste a color? I could. Medicine was *dope*! The wall of candy wrappers brought me into the world of sugar. Sweetness so intense it burned. Chocolate so earthy, you could feel the soil it grew on. The perfume bottles grew a garden—orchids, vanilla, lavender and other smells. I saw flowers, and a *whale* swam in an ocean of petals.

I must've been standing there for fifteen minutes straight, no lie. Everything spilled forth flavor. I ate and ate. Then I remembered where I was. Honestly, it was that grape soda smell that tickled my nose. That was his favorite flavor—that mix of natural flavors and chemicals. I could taste him, too. And I realized that if I stayed any longer, I might end up like him—a basement dwelling nigga with some kinda mutant disorder. I ran outta that room like a white girl in a horror movie.

I was hoping that this new thing I can do—taste everything— would stop or at least fade away. But it didn't. As I sit here, I can taste the paper and the damn ink. Mom thought I was sick or something. Dinner was too much for me. I mean, she made steak, right? I tasted blood and muscle and the shit they put in it to preserve it. It tasted wonderful and terrible. Each bite burned me. I tasted grass and gasoline, hay and stars. I saw the eyes of cows, brown and liquid like Coca Cola looking at me. I heard them singing to the earth, and felt the spike of pain as they were shot, and flesh ripped from their bones and sizzled up all nice and caramel on Mom's ancient frying pan that was seasoned by Nana's cooking. And don't get me started on the canned baby peas tasting of spring and aluminum. I told her that I'd eaten before. Which was true enough, if you thought about it.

September 12

Spoke to Nana again today.

Lemme speak to your Momma, she said, all serious.

I paused before I called out to Mom. *He called again, didn't he?* I said.

She didn't say nothing.

I called Mom to the phone.

September 18

Mom's been a real bitch. But I can't be too mad at her. Work at the hospital is bad, cause she has some asshole boss. And because of the bed bugs, she can't get any sleep.

At breakfast a couple of days ago I asked her what Nana had spoken to her about.

She didn't look at me. *This and that*, she said, looking into the cereal. The milk whispered with the voices of infants. The Cheerios stung me with the sweetness of wheat, the tang of chemicals. I almost didn't have to eat mine—I absorbed it somehow, like a sponge.

I said, *She told me that Daddy was looking for us*—

And she snapped. She told me to quit bothering her, she had to get ready for work. And that I should eat my damn breakfast, food costs money, you know.

I wasn't bothered by the bed bugs. Haven't been for days. Yesterday, I pulled up my mattress. It looked like a crime scene on the boxspring. All of the spicy, fruity smelling bugs had exploded.

September 22

I couldn't take it no more, so I went down to that nigga's room. It wasn't easy to find by sight. The halls in the basement twist and turn and the door is located in some sort of shadow space. But I found it by smell. I banged on the door.

What the hell did you do to me, I yelled through the closed door.

The door opened in a moment. He gestured me in.

I want this shit to stop, I said. *I ain't eating anything for a couple of weeks.* I'd begun to lose weight. My pants were not as tight as before. But—I wasn't hungry. The smell of everything drove me wild, and filled my stomach. Eating actual food seemed gross.

He didn't say nothing.

What's wrong with me, I said. *I am gonna become like you, a freaky Gollum-looking nigga?*

His glass teeth glittered and reflected the room, with its library of scent.

Come, he told me, without words.

I followed him out of the building. Down the loading dock, past the dumpsters, into the early evening. He walked in a funny way, always in the shadow. I found it easy to do that. Away from the street lamps, into blobs of darkness. It was like we were kids, trying to avoid the sidewalk cracks.

After a while, we didn't have to find the shadows. They *found* us. We walked by the river. Weeds, rats, empty 40s. Some young niggas were smoking blunts. Me and Shuggaman paused and hid in the shadows, drew them around us. We tasted it—the weed. Green and wild. I giggled, feeling it tickle my throat and my tummy.

One of the boys said, *You high?*

Another said, *Naw.*

And a third said, *This shit is bad. It don't work.*

Me and Shuggaman laughed in dark. We'd stolen all of the High from their reefer!

One of the boys said *You hear that?*

They looked by the tree line, squinting. They couldn't see us.

The two of us moved on, dark spot to dark spot, like fucked up children.

In an alley, we saw a homeless man eating a Kit Kat. Shuggaman waved me over to him. *Hide,* he said. *Eat.* It wasn't too hard to find shadows to step into. You just had to find the right angle. Soon I was behind this homeless nigga, eating his chocolate bar. I don't remember what I did, but suddenly, I was a sponge, absorbing all of the weird chemicals from his body. I could see them, sparkles in the air. They rose in glittering lines, toward me. And when I tasted I the sparkles....

I almost fainted. The sweetness was like lighting through my body. I felt like screaming. Maybe I did. My whole body sizzled. I must've looked like I was cumming. When I came to, I saw the homeless man in the alley crumpled into a ball. There was no more sugar in him. I don't know if he was breathing or not.

October 3

It probably was my fault. I can admit that now. But it wasn't *all* my fault.

I was walking in the hallway, minding my own business. My business: the smells and scents that drifted up, and fed me. The perfumes, the snacks, the liquor that Mr. Jackson drinks from his thermos, Shanté's Funyuns, lip gloss, Axe bodyspray. And sometimes, the jolt of sweetness from an open can of cola or gum. I saw colors, stories when I ate in this way. The whole world glowed and pulsated with rainbow shades. Even the shadows had colors.

So, I'm walking down the hallway, lost in the world when Kenyatta decides to get up all in my grill.

Look, it's Orca Winfrey, he says. And his trifling friends all laugh, like he's Chris Rock. I tried ignoring him. I swear I did. I walked on, heading toward my locker. He followed. I was sweating because it's so damn hot in this city. But he said I was sweating like a hog. *You look like you have bacon grease on you, Squasha.* He kept calling me fat, fat, fat. He pulled metaphors outta his ass. Fat like this, fat like that. Finally, I couldn't take it no more.

I pushed him against the locker. His crew said, *Oooooo* like a talk show audience.

Kenyatta just laughed.

So I bit him on the arm. I don't know why. It wasn't just that I was pissed at him. It was also that Kenyatta was surrounded by a cloud of colors and taste that I couldn't resist. He was like a damn bag of Skittles! My teeth broke through his skin easily, and the blood, sweet Jesus, it was so sweet. He lived on a diet of sugar and gum. I tasted it all. Not just white sugar, but other kinds. It filled my tongue. He was screaming and crying when a couple of his friends pulled me off him. He was on the floor quivering and saying, *That fat rabid bitch bit me.* I hated him saying that, so I put him to sleep. It was like I spoke to all the blood in his veins, and told it shut him down. And it obeyed me. His head drooped.

Someone said, *She killed him!*

I knew that I had to leave and soon. I pushed people outta the way and went to the bathroom.

Thank the lord, the bathroom was empty. I looked in the long wall mirror. I saw streaks of blood dripping down my face. I washed them off, but not before I caught a flash of something strange in the mirror.

My teeth. They were made of the same stuff as the mirror. They reflected. I also saw a flash of white in my hair. Was I getting darker? I couldn't tell in the flickering light of the bathroom.

I left school.

October 13

This is the last day of my life as Tasha. I won't need a name anymore. Or words. Words ain't nothing, not when the world is light, shadow, scent and taste. Getting a diploma, getting a job—what's that to an endless life of hunting? Money ain't nothing, compared to Sugar.

But here's what's worse: the sugarrush I got from that little taste of it. It was raw and wild. The taste gave me a headache. No wonder Shuggaman filtered the poisons through the air. Drinking it directly was like cola syrup before you added fizzy water.

I walked home, ignoring the nearly empty buses that passed by me. As I walked, I knew what I had to do. I could no longer live in the light, among people. I had to live with Shuggaman. He would teach me to love the dark. He would show me how to move between the rays of light and pools of shadow. He would teach me how to hunt, how to soothe people as I absorbed their poisons. I was crying as I walked across the Anacostia. Everyone ignored me. Who cares about a fat black girl?

When I got to our apartment building I ran into Miss Tammie. She was struggling with groceries. I helped her.

She said, *What you doing home from school so early? Couldn't wait to see your daddy, huh?*

I stopped. *What you mean, see my daddy?* I said.

She looked a little shocked herself, as if she'd said the wrong thing.

Your daddy's here. I let him in. I'm sorry. Maybe he wanted to surprise you and your momma.

It felt like someone had punched me in the stomach. I dropped the bag of hers I was carrying and ran to the elevator. I could hear her cussing at me. Thank baby Jesus that it came quickly, so I didn't have to deal with her bitching. It moved as slow as molasses, though. A thousand thoughts raced through my mind. Maybe he'd gotten better, stopped smoking...But that was stupid. Nana's phone calls...

When the doors opened to our floor, I could smell him. Sweat, iodine, salt, bleach... I could taste his madness. It tasted of the crack of dawn, sodium lights, pavement, rotten shoes, and endless need. I followed it like a trail. I could see where he'd jimmied the lock, the scraping of an animal.

I pushed open the door.

My daddy used to be strong, with dark, smooth skin. He had a nice bush, and a neatly trimmed moustache. The man at the window who turned at my entrance was thin, with ashy skin. There was blood on his knuckles. His hair was a mess and his mouth, when he opened it to smile at me, was a horror. He looked like someone had hit him with a bag of wet nickels.

Tasha, he said. It was a croak. *How you been, honey?*

What you doing here, I said.

He looked at me, confused that I wasn't all lovey dovey. I could feel his brain working, the gears grinding.

He said, *Why you leave and not tell me where you was.* He sucked his mouth. It was a dry sound, like he had no spit.

It's damn obvious.

Don't you talk to me like that, gal. He came toward me, shaking like a leaf. *What your momma say about me? She a lyin bitch.*

Don't talk about my momma like that.

He reached for me, but he could not grab me. It was second nature, slipping between light and shadow. It must've looked blurry. I smelled the rot from his breath, and beneath it, the chemical sugar, simmering. I felt all of his anger. It was jagged. He smacked me in the mouth, and I bit him. He fell into a trance almost immediately. Sleep, daddy, sleep. His blood was loaded with so much information, and tasted so delicious, that I could hardly pull myself from the red stream. I saw his nightmare journey across the country, looking for his wife and child. The back of Greyhounds, meals from vending machines, moments of chemical joy that shattered into endless aches of needing. I saw faces, including Nana's, policemen, dealers. There was so much there! But I moved away from it all, let him fall. And instead, I filtered the poison from him. I took it all: the meth and the sugar. I gorged myself on it. I saw it rise from him in a silver tissue haze, and it coated my tongue. It tasted like acid honey. It flowed into my mouth, and I drank until he was still, and his breath was calm.

Then I wrote a note:

Dear Momma, This is all my fault. You can blame me. I am sorry to leave him like this, but I got to go. Don't try to find me. Love, Tasha.

I left his body to cool on the carpet.

Inscribed

Hermes, Mercury: when you think of him, you doubtlessly see the fellow with wings on his cap and sandals. He is the messenger of the gods. Dig a little deeper, say, in Hamilton's retold myths, you get a sense of his trickster aspect. He becomes the god of thieves and nomads. But he also has other duties. He is a pyschopomp, one of those spiritual beings that leads the dead to their final resting place in Hades or the Elysian Fields. But this still does not complete the picture. He is also the god of change, a guardian of esoteric knowledge. He is the lord of magicians, the creator of writing. We get the word hermetic from him. His importance becomes more apparent when he is syncretized with the Egypt god Thoth. The ibis-headed god of scholars, magicians and symbols.

—Mercurial Magick: The Language
of Hermes and Thoth, Byron Davies

Simon knew that the funeral would be a circus. He'd prepared himself, mentally. But when he drove up the winding path, that resolve began to shift, ever so slightly. Maybe it was the sight of the first odd car on the road. A van painted with grapes in bunches. Maybe it was only a wine truck, but it something told him that it was something else, one of his father's kooky followers. Irene kneaded his shoulders. Simon jerked, then relaxed into her firm fingers that dug into his tense muscles.

The path to the place where the funeral was to be held was lined by evergreens. They didn't let the light in. His car chugged up the mountain road.

"The view is beautiful," Irene said, distracted.

Simon didn't reply; he was concentrating on the dusty road in front of him. When they reached the turn off where the lodge was, the trees fell away, dramatically revealing a view of the Blue Ridge Mountains and the valleys. An undulating sea of green below, endless blue sky above. He saw the lodge perched above the parking lot, a trapezoid of black done in a 70s style. And in the parking lot, the mourners emerged from their cars, not dressed in black.

Irene gasped, holding back a laugh.

Simon faced her, finally, and smiled. "I warned you."

They were mostly men, and to be fair, *some* of them were dressed in black. Nothing like the formal suit he wore now, but still respectful jackets and slacks in somber tones. But many, if not most, were dressed in tunics and sandals, looking like extras from *Gladiator*. Their hair was crowned with laurel leaves, or gold and silver circlets made to look like laurel leaves. He spotted a younger man dressed as a satyr, with horns glued onto his forehead. Another man wore a mask of gold, embossed with the ringleted hair of the ancients.

"I feel overdressed." Irene smoothed out her black dress and began to negotiate her pumps among the pebbles in the path. She gave his hand a squeeze. "I think we're the only straight people here," she whispered. She gave a sweet smile to a couple dressed as Castor and Pollux.

In the lodge, mourners mingled in the huge slate-floored meeting room. Among the eaves, bright green luna moths rested. There was a smell of incense, and, perhaps, another familiar smell. A tall man, dressed in a swirling wine-colored robe seemed to emerge from the shadows of the lodge. With his shaved head and severe features, Simon guessed that this was the master of ceremonies. Or priest. Or whatever.

"You must be Simon." His voice was softer than his look.

"Indeed. You must be Harvey Weinberg. And this is my—partner—Irene."

"You are welcome to say something about your father, after the service. If you are moved." Harvey placed his hand on Simon's arm. Simon was uncomfortably aware of the pressure there. *Did you fuck my father?* The ugly thought buzzed around his head. He swatted it away. He listened with a smile on his face as Harvey rattled on about the ceremony. Finally, Harvey left to gather the mourners. The smile—

which left him sore—fell from his face.

Irene had stood away while he'd spoken to the priest. She was speaking to the only other person of color at the gathering, besides themselves. He gave the brown-skinned man in a leather kilt a polite, apologetic smile, and steered Irene to a relatively secluded spot.

Simon whispered, "I don't think I can do this."

"What do you mean?"

"I mean, I can't...be here. I can't pretend that he was some great dad. I can't play that role..."

Irene stared at him. "You mean, just leave."

"I don't know..."

"Simon. We are not going to just leave." She paused, as if waiting for a protest. "If you leave, you'll feel even worse than you do now. Besides, I am not going to miss this for the world." She touched his face. He nodded.

A bell chimed, and silence fell upon the lodge. The procession began. Simon and Irene joined the group of men as they headed for the mountain's amphitheater. Tunics fluttered in the autumn air as they followed the path. There was a chill to the air. All was silent as they headed for the depression in the land where rounded benches spread out in a semi-circle. All of the seats faced a stage which had an altar draped with a deep purple cloth. A Grecian urn sat on this altar, surrounded by stalks starred with white and yellow blossoms. A man sat to the side, playing what was probably a lyre. It could have been a gathering of ancient Greeks, for all he knew. The only anachronisms were Irene and himself. And, perhaps, the printed programs lying on the pews.

There was an invocation to Hermes-Thoth. Then a glowing biography of Bryon Davies by Mr. Weinberg. This was a surreal pageant, compared to his mother's funeral a few years back. In fact, it was its polar opposite.

Viola Davies' funeral had been small, held in a church on H Street. Maybe 25 people showed up—it had been in the middle of a weekday, so that was understandable. Almost everyone there had been black, and dressed in their Sunday best. Her waxen body had rested at the front of the church, drowning in gardens of bouquets. Some woman, vying to be the next Fantasia, wailed over a gospel-inflected organ. It had been summer, and Simon had felt uncomfortable in his stiff suit. This was before he'd met Irene. He'd been alone. And of course, his father was nowhere in sight. Byron's stand-in had been a ladyslipper orchid, his mother's favorite flower. Byron had paid for the service and the repast. The very least he could do for a wife he'd left years ago.

Weinberg interrupted his reverie. "Now is the time to remember our brother, Byron Davies, as he was. I invite any who wish to share their remembrances. We will start with Byron's son, Simon."

Simon froze. He had no idea what he would say. He imagined facing the costumed, bejeweled, feathered freaks and telling them the story of how Viola Davies had been practically disowned from her family to marry a scrawny white scholar with no money or real prospects. How she used some of her own money to fund his Ph. D., only to be left when he gained recognition in his field. How Byron never visited her when she was dying of cancer. (He'd leave out the part where she explicitly told him not to visit her). These pretentious fags would gasp in horror—But the image of his mother, in her hospital gown, stopped him. Viola was proud; she was insistent that dirty laundry not be aired for the public to see. It was a relic of her upbringing in a prominent Washington family. No, he wouldn't embarrass her.

Irene tapped him on on the shoulder, and Simon became aware of the expectant and mostly white faces gazing at him. He stood up, and made his way to dais. He stood next to his father's ashes. He couldn't face these people, so he focused instead on Irene, who gave him an encouraging glance.

The words seem to come of their own volition.

"I learned pretty early on that Dad wasn't like other dads." (There was some light laughter; he hadn't intended that, but it made sense). "You see, while other dads taught their kids to ride bikes or play ball, my father taught me mythology. But they weren't myths to him; they were real. When I was young, the Minotaur, and the Furies and Zeus were as real to me as Santa Claus and the Easter Bunny. Forget Bugs Bunny cartoons and the Transformers and Star Wars; he gave me Apollo, Echo and Narcissus, and yes, Hermes and Thoth. When I was little, the monsters in the closet were the harpies and many nights I'd wake up thinking that Scylla was lurking beneath my bed...

"He didn't just give me stories, though. Even during the time that he and Mom broke up, we kept in touch... He'd send coded messages to me..."

They came back to him, those missives on gray paper scrawled with Byron's distinctive chicken scratch. Acrostics and cryptograms and other linguistic puzzles. At first, he ignored them. He was firmly on Team Viola. But gradually—with his mother's urging—he kept in touch with Byron, took the bait. Letters sent back to whatever address he was at—a series of shifting college posts, lover's houses, and some overseas retreats.

Someone coughed in the amphitheater, someone with a mask of gold. It knocked Simon out of his reverie. He finished hastily, and allowed other people to share their remembrances. Most were respectful, but there was one person who began to share an off-color adventure he'd had with his father—involving mushrooms, a bathhouse in Athens and a young Greek Tadzio—that set him on edge. After the remembrances, Weinberg took the urn off the dais and invited people to follow to the edge of a cliff. Below, there was a sea of green trees. They rustled in the breeze. A prayer was spoken, and the priest turned the urn upside down.

Grey ashes scattered down to the ground below. It started as a massive cloud, and slowly dispersed until he could no longer tell the difference between his father's remains and the pollen.

INSCRIBED

Every culture has them: Gods or beings that act as guides to the spirit making a transition from being housed in living flesh to being untethered. The god will come and gather the wandering spirit and lead it to its final resting ground: Heaven, Hell, the Elysian Fields, the underworld....In Christianity, that role is filled by St. Peter, the judge at the Pearly Gates. Odin, among his other responsibilities, performs this service in the Norse Pantheon, and in Vodoun, the top-hatted specter Papa Legba is the escort...
—*Mercurial Magick: The Language of Hermes and Thoth*, Byron Davies

As he closed his eyes for the last time, he heard the whispering darkness. When he opened them, he saw the inscribed man. The man was nude, with dark skin, but inscribed with silvery green ink. He tried to look at the man's face. He couldn't focus on it—words and reflections distorted the features. He wasn't even sure what he saw in the brightness was even a properly human face. But it didn't matter anyway. The place where he and the man were began to fall apart, and he—and the inscribed man—both fell.

Darkness that stretched forever. A tunnel. He followed the shining creature, sometimes walking, sometimes falling, and sometimes floating. It seemed to take forever. But he didn't notice the passage of time. It was meaningless here, as was his name. There was only the need to follow. Nothing to see. The tunnel or hole was featureless. There was only dark. No warmth, no cold. No fear, or hunger. Just the silver-green man...

And then he is here, where ever here is. There is no inscribed man. But silver is everywhere. The ground, the sky, the mountains in the distance, all is silver. The nodding fields of wheat, the sprays of tiny flowers, all moon-colored. He is in a landscape in negative. He walks through the field, looking for—what? He is alone in this new place.

He begins to walk in the landscape, through fields of silver wheat. A breeze combs through the land. The sky does not change. No bird, no cloud mars the expanse of pale silver. Didn't the sky used to be another color?

At this thought—brief and niggling as it is—the sky changes. A dark color spills from the edges, like ink spills across paper. It stains the silver, erases it. A rich cobalt sky bleeds above him. He smiles. And the silver wheat becomes golden. The silver-white flowers are turn bright yellow, and the circle of a sun blooms in the new sky.

This feels right. He walks on, not feeling any urgency or feeling tired. The wheat almost parts before him, it is so soft. It closes behind him, clearing away the path he has made. This does not disturb him, but the silence does. And suddenly, there are sounds. The breeze stirring the wheat, the crunch of seed-heads beneath his feet. He glances up in to the sky, and sees birds circling above him. They have black and white feathers, and narrow sickles for beaks.

He pauses in his journey. It's as if—as if the land is creating itself around him. He thinks: mountains. And in the distance are purple, cloud-wreathed cones of jagged rock. The realization hits him, of his current state, of where he is.

The sterile white hospital. The bleeping instruments that monitored his impending death. The fluids that dripped in ruined veins, the tubes, the gleaming canisters, the hovering nurses in scrubs with childish patterns...It all comes back to him. His name comes back to him, along with memories. Byron knew he was dying when he saw the man in the corner of his room. Doctors and nurses scurried around his bed as one machine or another whined. He found himself standing and staring at the shape. Byron glanced casually at the body in the bed. It—him—was wrecked, a thing of bodily fluids and meat. Why were the hospital staff trying so hard to resurrect such a ruined, rotten thing? It was futile. He watched as the obscured man in the corner of room, who, like him, was calm and serene, became clearer, his features resolved. Fully formed, the man in the corner wore a tunic that was dyed purple. Wings were on his golden sandals. Byron was filled with excitement. The man's sacred name hovered at his lips. Then he saw the face of the man. It disturbed him. First, the skin was darker than he'd expected the figure's skin to be; it had a deep bistre color. The hair was close-cropped and tightly curled. And the face and features...He knew them from somewhere. Then the man began to glow silver, the hospital and the world fell away.

Gurgles in the distance. Water over rocks. When he comes to the end of the wheat field he sees it flashing in the distance, a river of white water snaking around. On the other side are temples with Ionic columns and statues cloaked in ivy bloom like stone flowers. There is movement along the banks of the chattering river, people. Maybe a hundred of them. Most of the men and women look dazed. They are lost, as he is.

When he finally reaches the banks of the river, the crowd on its banks are all staring down, transfixed by the water. They no longer are lost; they are just silent figures staring in the swirling depths. Curious, Byron stares into the water. It is iridescent and shimmering, as if made of liquid opal. Colors flow past, ribbons of metallic pink and green and blue. In between the water sparkles, reflects. He sees his own face, clear from illness and age. The smoothness of his skin is a marvel. Then, he begins to see other faces....

Alchemy is often mistaken for the simplistic act of turning base material into gold. Alchemy, in actuality, refers to the process of transformation, and the "gold" at the end is metaphorical. Words are the ultimate base material, which reaches its golden state by being written down—captured thought. What is a more potent spell?

—*Mercurial Magick: The Language of Hermes and Thoth*, Byron Davies.

Simon woke up to a thick, congealed darkness. Not even the digital numbers glowing on the alarm clock could penetrate the gloom, so he waited patiently for the room to resume its familiar shapes. His mind was filled with the ragged edges of dreams. He tried to blink the images away. A landscape of ruins in startling gray. A river drenched in color, full of disembodied faces that were trapped in a current... He assumed that Byron's funeral had summoned these dreams. He was pissed at his subconscious; he didn't really give a crap about Dad. It was maddening to know that in some far off region of his brain that he did care. Irene breathed softly next to him; she was a tangle of dreadlocks and pillows. When his vision felt comfortable enough, he stepped quietly from the room.

The living room was lit by the yellow streetlights outside. Even on the sixth floor, the sound of the Adams Morgan late night crowd drifted up to his window. Squealing taxicabs, voices in slurred English, Spanish and Amharic, and bits of music—salsa and HipHop—drifted up to his window. He bypassed the couch, with its inviting throw and abandoned novel for the desk, where his computer sat. Next to the computer was his father's magnum opus, *Mercurial Magick*. Irene had probably left it there. He hadn't been very forthcoming about his father—she only knew his father as a Famous Scholar and was searching for clues about him.

"He sounds insufferable," Irene had said on their third date, when he'd finally told her about his family. "Does he wear a monocle and speak in Latin to you?"

"Just about," Simon said. "It got worse when he left my mother. He became a kind of gay shaman."

Irene had laughed. "Is there any other kind?" She had the touch of high priestess about her, with her batiked blouse and cowrie shells studded in her dreads.

Simon now flipped through the book; he had to admit it was handsome volume. The cover showed an ibis-headed man writing hieroglyphics on a sheet of papyrus. The title was embossed in gold-leaf. The endpapers were splashed with celestial charts, and the pages were ragged-edged. There was a kind of spell-book feel to it, which accounted for its massive popularity among the New Age crowd. Simon recalled the myths his father told him. They were unedited and not kid-proofed for him—which made them all the more wonderful. Zeus's Captain Kirk-like libido filled his young mind—the dalliances with swans and his shape-shifting into rays of light or bulls. Gilgamesh and Enkidu were more exciting to him than Superman or Batman. His nightmares were decorated with Byron's vivid tales that featured one-eyed Gods, snake-haired maidens, and bloody underworlds. Simon put the book down. Byron was a bastard of the highest order. A douche. And it had nothing to do with his hidden sexuality. It had to do with the fact that he was a user. While he dreamed and wrote about long forgotten gods, his mother supported the two of them with crappy jobs. True, Byron got a stipend when he was writing his thesis, but it was Viola who paid for things like food and made sure that there was a roof over their head. They followed Byron across the country, to adjunct and associate positions, in one bedroom apartments and once, a glorified dorm room. And as soon as he got what he wanted—tenure and academic acclaim— he left them high and dry.

Out of boredom, he woke up the computer. Instead of the familiar screensaver (a slide show of he and Irene in Barbados lounging on the beach), there was a bleak landscape in black and white. Ruined temples and headless statues littered the fields. In the distance, a river flashed. The screensaver was slightly animated. A breeze rippled the the grasslands.

Simon shivered. There was some resonance here; he'd seen this place. But when? He'd have to ask Irene why she'd changed the screensaver,

The screensaver faded for longer than usual when he moved the mouse. The dissolve effect seemed to move pixel by pixel. It was probably some malware. He played solitaire for an hour or so, robotically moving cards across an emerald background. The cards danced across the screen every time he won. He waited until his eyes blurred. He did a quick check of his email—nothing new but a few condolences, and a bunch of spam. As he put the computer to sleep, he saw—briefly, weirdly— that strange landscape flash on screen. The screen turned dark before he could be sure.

The Greek underworld is a grey place, full of bleak beauty. The soul here

is lost, wandering a melancholy landscape free of memory or context. Only those whose crimes are so heinous—such as Prometheus or Sisyphus—received "special" treatment. The underworld was the ultimate purgatory.
—Mercurial Magick.

The faces slip by too quickly. He recognizes them, but the names that go with the faces dance just out of reach. Was that man with the square jaw and steel blue eyes his father—or his grandfather? And that woman with the blond chignon with the beauty mark on her right cheek his mother—or some aunt? Byron finds that he doesn't really care all that much. There is a brief flare of wistful regret that is also washed away by the current. Gradually the silver-white water stops offering faces. Simultaneously, the current slows to a sluggish trickle. His own reflection returns, and the water mirrors the still sky. Byron stands, and surveys the other side of the river.

Statues as pure white as the moon. Temples inlaid with green and black marble. Fields of flowers that ripple with breezes and butterflies. Something was different about that side of the shore. Hadn't it been a little more...desolate? It didn't matter. He had to get to the other side.

He doesn't see a bridge or any other method of crossing the river. He watches as an old woman, bent by age staggers into the shallow depths of the almost still water. The water strips away her clothing, like an acid. But her skin is kept intact for the most part. Blue varicose veins melt away, as do her wrinkles the deeper she goes into the water. Images flash in the water, presumably scenes from her life. Children, lovers and places pass by in hummingbird-quick ripples. Then she's submerged in the deep center of the water. He waits for her to emerge on the other shore. After a minute or two, he sees something, a faint wispy form ascending from the waters. A woman shaped of dew. She fades into the landscape.

Byron steps into the water, eager to follow her example. The water is birth-warm and comforting. The feel of it between his toes and legs is enticing, lulling. He feels parts of himself—his memories—spilling out into concentric circles on the water, stretched to the edge, stilled. Will he lose his name when his head goes beneath the surface? Byron finds that he doesn't much care. And down his head goes, into the tepid water.

"Byron."

The water turns opaque. No smooth stones, but jagged rocks that cut his feet. Moss, slime, sediment and mud ooze by him.

"Byron."

The ruined voice sounds around him and in his head. The ticklish touch of a frond of seaweed; he turns around, and faces her. She is gaunt, with shriveled features. Her dark skin has a cast of ash about it, and her eyes are dull. Her lips are cracked, in spite of being submersed in murky, milky water. She is bald, and wears the hospital gown she probably died in. Her throat, dear Lord, her throat is a wreck. A piece has been torn out of it, so that he sees blackened meat where the cancer swarmed and destroyed. Water flows in and out out of the voice box. Some creature— an eel?—peeks up from the void.

Byron screams, and his mouth fills with water. But instead of erasing memory, the water reconstructs them, meticulously. Every terrible thing that's ever happened to him. Every terrible thing that he's ever done.

"Say my name," she says. Cigarette ash, chemotherapy, tracheotomy plug, the scent of radiated flesh all surround her. The voice has a dry sound—rubbed raw and crusted wounds. "Say it, you old fool."

"Viola," he whispers. The current drags it away.

His wife, the one he left for—what? Paganism? His love of other men? Or academic fame? Viola has come back, full of anger. *Vengeance.*

"Viola," he begins, softly, "you must know that I have always loved you. I had to leave because—"

"Quiet. Stop trying to placate me. I have neither desire nor the time. You must listen to me."

Once he got beyond her ghoulish appearance, he recognizes the headstrong ferocity he loved. It was the voice of the girl who dared anyone to speak about their risqué interracial relationship, to the point of confrontation. There was one time when they were in a restaurant in DC where an old redneck had...

"Pay attention. Don't drift away." Viola's voice was sharp, almost militaristic. It snapped him—immaterial jetsam wisp—back to focus.

"You woke something. In your studies. It does not live, but it wants to live again."

"What do you mean?"

"That damned god you worshiped."

It takes him a moment to absorb this information. And when he does, warmth suffuses throughout his body. It was like a love affair, chasing the scraps of myth and philosophy, weaving them together. The creator of language and magic; the lord of thieves and travelers; winged helm and ibis-headed. It all makes sense now. Death is not an ending; it is the path to divinity. The Divinity.

Viola curses. It is an ugly sound—scraped raw. She never cursed in life. But that fact makes her obscenity more obscene. She curses him, and then, curses the god. The blasphemy has an effect. She begins to crumble, like a clod of dried mud. The current begins to crush her fragile body.

"Stop," she gasps. A cheek fractures. "It..." Some organ, dried and useless, escapes from her hospital gown. "Simon..."

The last word she says destroys her. Ears and eyes detach. Teeth and bones are borne away by the river.

Hermes is credited with the creation of a magical language. A lexicon that transforms reality, an alphabet that produced omens. The stories of how he came to this arcane knowledge are lost.

Hermes, of course, is also the god of thieves....

—Mercurial Magick.

"Simon," Irene said.

He looked up from the screen. "Yeah?"

She looked pissed—pursed lips, arms folded. Cautiously, "What's wrong?"

"You know how many times I've been calling you?" She'd tied her dreads back into a kind of bun-ponytail hybrid. Strands escaped the elaborate knotting.

Simon was tempted to be sarcastic, and hazard a guess. But that would be the wrong move—humor wouldn't appease her. He played it straight. "No, how many?"

"Seven. Seven times."

He didn't say anything. He waited for her next move.

She unfolded her arms, turned around. "You didn't use to be like this."

"Like what?"

She made a sound of annoyance—an in-drawn breath, sharp.

"Irene?"

"Never mind," she said, walking into the kitchen.

"I..." He stopped. It was no use. Best to let her cool down.

He turned back to the computer.

"Goddammit, Simon!"

He turned back to see Irene sitting at the table. The smells of roast chicken, buttered rice and green beans wafted up to him. His stomach rumbled; he was famished.

He moved away from the computer, after putting it to sleep. "What's wrong," he said.

"You, asshole. I've been calling you to dinner for five minutes. And you acted like you couldn't hear me."

"Sorry. I guess I was... "

What *was* he doing?

"Yeah, well. Next time, *you* make dinner. I've been doing it all week." Irene served herself, and pushed the rest of the serving dishes to him, a bit roughly. They ate in silence for a few minutes.

He said, "I don't know when I began playing that game. I don't remember buying it, or downloading or anything. But it just, you know, it's just addictive, I guess. I'm sorry that I've been so out of it." He paused, savoring the food.

Irene moved rice around her plate, made a hill of rice. A dreadlock broke free, fell on her shoulder. She said, "It doesn't really look like anything. It just looks like a bunch of flashing lights. Great graphics though. What's it called?"

"That's the thing, Irene. I don't know. I mean, it has no title. It's just...there."

"How's that even possible? And what's the point of the game? It is like, role playing or like Donkey Kong or what?"

"It's hard to describe. It's kind of like a puzzle, of sorts. You solve one piece, and then you move on. And you solve another... And it's kind of like, I don't know, a travelogue. You get see all these cool things. Optical illusions, things like that."

"But there's no music. "

"Right."

"Let me play it," she said, finally.

Something stirred in him, some dark emotion. He didn't want her to play the game or what ever it was. It was his, his alone. It was private. But he ignored the strange emotion, or tried to. As he cleared the table and started doing the dishes, he did his best not think about her playing with his—*their*—computer. A glass went into soapy water, and emerged clothed in iridescent bubbles. It slipped out of his hand, back into the sink and she probably messed up my place. Though he couldn't tell what that place was.

He forced himself to do the dishes slowly, without thinking about the game. But it was impossible. The water glasses reminded him of the urns that he'd had to search in, during one segment. He was searching for something, and finding feathers or stones or vipers or bees instead, until he finally found the thing he was (apparently) looking for: a tablet splashed with glyphs. The china dishes he dried had a pattern reminiscent of a detail in a piece of fabric he'd had to find some other piece of hidden text on. (Not that the text made any sense; the letters were from some nonsense alphabet).

When he was finished, Simon found Irene had closed the computer, and was reading a magazine article. He quashed the urge to open up the laptop.

"Well," he said.

She looked up from her article. "I don't see what you see in it. I mean, the graphics are cool. But I couldn't figure it out. And—it's not an English game. I mean, American. It's like was made in Albania or something. I couldn't recognize the writing."

"What did you see?"

She thought for a moment. "It was kind of creepy. I was walking through some kind of forest grove. It was all rendered lovingly. It was very Mediterranean—cypress trees, lemon trees, low shrubs, that sort of thing. I was just wandering and wandering. Almost like it wasn't a game, but—as you said—a kind of computerized travelogue. There's no music, but, there is ambient sound. Rustling leaves. Crunching underfoot. And there's a sense that someone is chasing you. Leisurely. As if he could pounce at any moment...

"I walked through that forest for a while, looking for something, anything—while trying to avoid the guy or whatever, for a whole day, until evening came, in the game's time. Finally, I came to a monolith or whatever, covered with that weird writing. It glowed. But I knew if I approached it, that the person following me would strike. I just *knew* it. That's when I stopped playing. I don't like 'mindfuck' games."

He paused before continuing. "So, you kind of see why I'm kind of interested in it."

"Oh yeah. It's addictive as crack. And like crack, it can screw you up, too. Do me a favor. See if you can stay away from it. Just for a little while. Let's say, a couple of days. You think you can do that?"

Simon glanced at the closed computer. The compulsion to explore the environment thrummed through his arms. His fingers ached to be on the keyboard.

"I think I can manage that," he said.

He knew it was a lie even as the words left him.

It ascends from the earth to the heaven. It extracts the lights from the heights and descends to the earth containing the power of the above and the below
—Trans from the Tabula Smaragdina (Emerald
Tablets of Hermes Trismegistus)

Dreaming, he walks through the landscape. Symbols are everywhere, like insects. He must decipher them. He annotates everything.

A river flows by and he feels endlessly sad. Drowning in sorrows. And as he remembers all that he would miss on earth, a name floats up in his brain, a bubble of knowledge. The river's name: Archeron.

In naming the river, his sorrow dissipates. And he finds himself elsewhere.

Elsewhere is a field of beautiful young men. Half-nude, they stretch and run and fight amongst themselves. Byron remembers the contraband muscle magazines he'd hidden beneath his bed when he was young, with their images of bronzed muscle gods. He watches the youths' rough and tumble games, beyond arousal. He speaks the name of the place aloud.

He is whisked away.

How long does he stumble through the underworld? There is no way of knowing.

Each river, ruined temple, flower is a clue. The bird warbles a note that reminds him of.... That portico has faded words in a language he once knew...

"Wake up," Viola says, her voice a rasp. He smells her before he sees her: meat and blood and rotting things. In a clap of wings and scrape of claws, she lands before him, on a rock in some wood. She has some of her beauty back, skin a healthy brown, her hair the Afro she never wore in life. Her breasts are full, globular. But the rest of her is feathered and clawed. Something that's dying wriggles in one of her claws. The red on her mouth is not lipstick.

"If you do one thing right, you old faggot, you'll do this." Byron shivers at her harsh word choice. "How long have wandered this grey hell, looking for cock?"

"Spare me. Each moment you lollygag, that thing is ensnaring your son. But maybe you don't care about that." Her claw casually cracks the skull of the creature—rabbit?—it was holding. Brain and bone spatter and seep into the old pine needles. Byron's incorporeal stomach turns at the visual. He finds this atavistic Viola terrifying...and enticing. She continues: "I suppose, because you couldn't screw him, or that he is too dark, you don't care. He's not you're type—"

"Stop it! I do care about him. Remember, I used to have him in the summers—"

"—Then prove it, dammit. Save him, from that thing you woke, that *pyschopimp*."

"Psychopomp, Viola. The word is psychopomp."

There is a pause, the space of a breath. Then, they both laugh—the disembodied spirit and the lamia.

Viola ends the moment by gnawing on the carcass, smearing her face with gore.

Byron sighs. "Can you help me?"

She pauses her feeding. "I don't belong here. I will try, though. I can only take over creatures momentarily."

"Do you know where to find the—god?"

She stops eating. "I quite like this form." She flutters her dark pinions.

"Viola?"

"Oh, yes. There is a place, a monolith. That is the apex of the game Simon is playing. I suspect that's where you'll find...it." She spat out a bone. "Follow me."

She takes to the air, razoring through the forest's canopy.

Its father is the sun, its mother the moon.
—*Trans from Tabula Smaragdina (Emerald Tablets of Hermes Trismegistus)*

Years ago, he'd visited Byron at a commune in Vermont for the summer. Simon was thirteen, and the heat of his parent's divorce was cooling. Viola wanted him to go; she'd insisted. Simon hadn't seen him for a couple of years. There was just the occasional phone call and letter—both of which he'd barely acknowledged. Monosyllables and grunts were his preferred communication method. In fact, he suspected his sullen attitude was his mother's main motivation to get him out of DC and the house.

He listened to Chuck D rap about white supremacy on his Walkman in the back of the sage-scented silver Volvo driven by Theo, Dad's current partner. Theo had curly blond hair and the feathery beginnings of facial hair. He always wore black, even when it was 100 degrees outside, and smoked clove cigarettes. He wore tiny circular spectacles. When Byron—and at the time, he was Byron, and not Dad—introduced the two of them at the airport—Theo had made the mistake of trying to hug him. Simon jumped back. There was a moment when he seriously considered decking the pale *faggot*. And that was the word that came to his head, unbidden—faggot. Simon stopped himself; that would be going too far.

In spite of the dread he felt, Simon enjoyed the drive up to the commune. The weather was hot but not as humid as it was in DC. The hills rolled by, covered by dense forests and interrupted by farmhouses. Cows munched grass stupidly by the road. Hermetica, the commune, was deep within one of these forests, down a dusty dirt road. Simon regretted wearing his Air Jordans—they were white and pristine, like he always kept them. That would be impossible now. Shit.

The gravel parking lot was full of VWs and vans. Dirty-looking hippies strolled around the woods. As he suspected, they were all white, burned by the sun, with peeling skin. Women were in Birkenstocks and those lose flowing sheet-like dresses that hid their bodies. Many of the men had long hair they kept in untidy ponytails—while their receding hairlines crept further and further up their skulls.

"We're here," Byron announced.

"Looks like the damn Spahn Ranch," Simon muttered.

He thought he heard Theo laugh.

After settling in his father's cabin (thank God or whoever Byron worshiped, Theo wasn't staying there), they went to the communal dinner, which was held in a long house that made Simon think that he'd been transported back into the time of Vikings. The wooden roof was high and raftered, and anchored at one end with a gigantic fireplace. The hundred or so people sat at mahogany picnic tables and ate mostly vegetarian fare—bulgur wheat, roasted root vegetables—and plain water. Simon filled up on bread, which was dense and looked like it had at least 4 million grains. He loaded it up with the soft goat cheese and briny olives that were on the table. He couldn't wait to leave—he knew that he'd loose weight at the end of the two weeks. The thin, red and pink speckled white people looked at him like he was an exotic animal.

Most of his stay at Hermetica was spent listening to music—he learned *Fear of a Black Planet* by heart—and long walks in the woods. He mostly avoided Byron; his father was always writing or teaching a lecture on ancient Greece or alchemy or some other bullshit. People treated Byron like he was some reborn Greek god himself, and Theo followed Byron around like a puppy dog.

One time, during one of his walks, it began to rain. It was a deluge, bowing branches and the earth was a river of mud in minutes. Simon ran back through downpour, splashing and jumping through puddles until he finally reached Byron's cabin. He made a beeline for the bathroom, when he heard a sudden gasp that came from the bedroom. Simon both knew—and didn't know—what that sound was. The gasp came again. Dad's voice—it sounded like when he'd get charley-horses. Then, there was a second voice that said, "Oh, Jesus," but not in an angry way. And it was Theo. It took a moment before Simon realized what was probably going on in the bedroom.

He stepped out into the rain. It pounded on him. He didn't care. He didn't think. He didn't want to do either—care or think. He just walked in mud and rain until the rain stopped. He ruined his Air Jordans. But they didn't seem to matter so much. He slipped in the cabin during dinner hour and changed. No-one seemed to care when he came in late.

Oh, Byron made a half-hearted attempt: "Where were you? We were getting worried."

Simon muttered some lie about being stuck out in the rain. But images of Theo and Dad naked danced around his head. He sullenly ate the macrobiotic or some such shit food, trying to quell the inappropriate thoughts in his head. He started singing the lyrics to A Tribe Called Quest's *Bonita Applebaum*. That dinner lasted forever.

There was only one other event of note during that torturous visit. One night, the entire group at Hermetica—mostly pagans and self-styled shamans—gathered in a clearing during the full moon. The moon was fat, round and yellow, like a wheel of Vermont cheddar. Trees and leaves seemed to strain towards it. It was breezy and cool enough for a jacket. Simon had left his behind in the cabin, and was shivering slightly in his Bugs Bunny as a B-boy t-shirt. The women mostly wore Holly Hobbie dresses and shawls. Dad was in a black turtleneck, and the hippie men seemed to favor ponchos.

The grass in the field grew high. One of the women, dressed in a simple black dress with a bad perm sprouting from her head, stood barefoot on a boulder, and raised her arms to the sky, as if she wanted to hug the moon.

She said, in a high, squeaky voice, "All hail, Artemis!"

Simon did his best to stop laughing. The look Theo shot him was pure rage.

The gathered group murmured hail to the cheese-moon. And the whole thing was cheesy.

Who the hell did they think they were? It was bad enough that his father was homosexual; conceivably, Simon could deal with that. (In time). But this worship was...silly. Some of the hippies brought drums. They began to pound on them with crude rhythms. His father stood and started quoting something or other from 'the Emerald Tablets.' Simon thought he smelled weed. Mom would have a fit when he told her about that. (If he told her). Some people began to sway, others rattled gourds.

Simon had enough of this. He didn't belong here. It was only a matter of time before he started laughing at these people and their pathetic displays. What did they think was gonna happen? In the frenzy, he stood and started to slip away. He thought he could remember the path back to the main area. He had a flashlight and the moon was bright.

The forest canopy, however, blotted most of the moon's light out, and the light his flashlight gave out was feeble. Still, the path was clearly delineated and it was a, what, ten, fifteen minutes tops back walk to the compound? He followed a path, drifted further away from the ritual back there. In no time at all, he heard nothing but the crunch of his ruined Air Jordans on mud, leaves, branches and probably some raccoon shit. Now and then moonlight broke through the cover, making weird shapes in the distance. About ten minutes passed before Simon began to think that maybe he'd been mistaken and was, in fact, lost. Surely the resident cabins and long house weren't this far out. But he hadn't really been paying attention, had he? There'd been a younger hippie girl who was acceptable looking, with long dark hair and swollen breasts that moved beneath her shirt's thin fabric that he'd been concentrating on. She smelled nice... Now, he recalled that there were many paths throughout Hermetica. He'd just gotten on the wrong one. No big deal. He would just trace his steps back to clearing. Simon turned and backtracked. It was noticeably silent here. He could hear his own breath. No matter. He'd soon hear that crazy earth-biscuit chanting soon enough. But the silence went on just a tad longer than he expected. Which was fine, because, at the worst, he could wait until sunrise and then find his way back. Besides, what was in these woods, anyway? Black bears, coyotes. But they were rare, right? Simon laughed. He was freaking himself out. He was still on a clear path, made by humans. If he was lost, he wasn't that lost.

All the same, horror movie scenarios played in his brain. The hook-handed, ski-masked killer, slicing bodies with a blood-slicked machete... Simon knew that the black guy was the first to die. Man, he hated this commune, and Hermetica. Why did Mom have send him away from the city and his friends, with all of these crazy white people? He still moved on, trying not to think about murderers or wild animals, or the fact that his flashlight would flicker every now and then. He'd walk for five more minutes and then began to call for help. He didn't care if he disturbed the ritual or not. Or—maybe he would tell them that he'd been lead away from the camp by a goatman or that Artemis herself had appeared and beckoned him with her hounds.

He laughed nervously when he thought of the awed faces of the commune members when he told them the lie. Something answered his laugh. A low growl of something. Simon waved the flashlight around wildly. It jittered, and sparked off something, a pair of green eyes in a tree. The shape of the green-eyed creature looked like nothing he'd ever seen before, nothing he thought was possible. It crouched like a cornered cat, but was long with tapered snout like a weasel. It thrashed its tail and bared its teeth. Simon backed away, and began to run. He tripped a few moments later over something. He felt the flashlight slip from his hand as the ground rose up to meet him.

A thousand things hit Simon at once: pain, cold, the rotten smell of the ground. There was no light, save the sliced-up moon and starlight; the cheap-ass flashlight was busted. He lay still for a minute, convincing himself that he wasn't dead or too hurt. He tried to get up, and found that his front palm was gashed. Other than a banged knee he was OK. He hoped that the strange weasel-cat was gone. He started to walk, and found that he'd gone from the path when he'd began to run. He considered calling for help, but he thought he might attract something other than the commune folk. He waited. He heard nothing. "Help," he said, a croak, finding his voice. "Help!" He no longer cared if he interrupted their sacred nonsense or not. Screw them. Everyone knew that the Greeks stole things from Africa, anyway...It was all a lie, nonsense.

He called out a few more times, each time getting louder. Surely, someone heard him. But maybe they were too deep in their trance, drunk on hemlock-tainted Kool-Aid. Their heads up their asses...A twig snapped in nearby. Simon started. And he heard footsteps in darkness. His heart stopped. A dark form parted the trees, and moved towards him. At first Simon didn't care who it was—it could have been Theo and he would have been happy. But there was something strange about the man. Something moved on him. His clothes glittered with some glow-in-the-dark substance. Letters, and shapes shifted. It was a cool shirt, one that changed frequently. And the light was kind of green.

"Thank god," said Simon. "I thought I was lost. I saw a wolverine or something..."

The man turned and began walking away, slowly. He didn't turn back. Simon shrugged, and followed.

The man with glowing shirt—and, as it turned out, pants—led him on no discernible path. Branches and bushes and brambles where everywhere, but Simon found that the going was easy, almost as if the dark wood bent to his guide's will. The man with spinning letters that glowed like neon led him silently forward. Yellow moon, dark wood and neon-splashed man were all Simon knew for a while. He wanted to speak to him, but he didn't dare. They moved through the wood. Were they alone? It didn't feel like it. Simon felt spidery tingles on his back. Turning back, he could see bodies fading in trees. Once, he glimpsed a woman, black against the misty gray of the forest. She looked immeasurably sad, and she was nude. Simon didn't look back after that and instead kept his eye on the man whose clothes had glowing symbols on it. Simon had to keep him in sight; the man moved silently. Finally, they reached the clearing where the commune was still gathered. They were still listening to Byron blather on about something or other. Probably hadn't noticed he'd gone. Simon moved back to where he'd been sitting. He turned to the forest where the man had been. He was gone, of course.

Simon ended up dozing, and had to be woken up by Theo. He almost told him about his adventure in the woods—but then remembered the sounds in the cabin.

He kept an eye out for his mysterious rescuer, but he never saw him the rest of the time there. He found that he didn't care that much. He only wanted to see his shirt again, with the cool glowing letters. Simon began copying them from memory on paper. The curves and lines, loops and circles. The shapes, which hinted at sound. They looked like some kind of formula. He learned new words for graphic symbols, and found himself drawing them as he listened to his Walkman. Tildes, asterisks, six-pointed stars. Infinity signs, alphas and omegas. Unsurprisingly, Hermetica's library was filled with encyclopedias of them. It was a good way to pass the time, anyway.

One time, Dad caught him doing it.

"What are you working on?"

"Just some sh— Nothing. Just doodles."

"It looks like—almost like—Alchemical symbols..."

"It's nothing. Nothing." And Simon shut Byron out.

Simon shut Irene out, or at least he tried to. But Irene, being Irene, wasn't having it.

One day after dinner, before he hopped onto the computer and the strange game, she said, "I think you're grieving."

"What?" He was collecting the dishes and silverware, and heading to the galley-style kitchen.

"You're grieving," she repeated. "I'm no therapist, but come on. Burying yourself into some weird computer game, collecting symbols. The whole obsession thing. It's like you're becoming like him."

"You're crazy," he said, and turned on the faucet.

"Yeah. I'm crazy. And you're just spending days and nights playing some sort of game based on alchemy and magic words. That uses *Greek* symbols."

"I—it doesn't just use Greek symbols. The game is relaxing. And anyway, that's just a coincidence. Lots of games use those symbols. They all aren't obsessed with Byron Davies."

She sucked her teeth. Then let a single, under-the-breath, "mmm—mmmh" escape from her mouth.

Whatever. Let her believe her New Age post Oprah psychoanalytic theory. He went back to the dishes, and lost himself in the drudgery of soap, hot water, and Fiestaware.

(He was glad that Irene didn't look in the bag he'd bought home from work. In it was a notebook, filled with his notes about the game).

Simon had done some research during work, when he was supposed to be designing brochures, and found information about it. The game was called *Trismegistus*, and had been designed by someone named Theodore A. Marcus. (Surely not *that* Theo)? It had followed the fate of many computer games—into oblivion, with a few faithful cultists resurrecting it in abandonware game sites in the further reaches of the web. How it found its way to him, he wasn't sure. Anyway, he was not alone in his obsession, not by far. Like *Myst*, *Trismegistus* was an inscrutable puzzle game. Unlike *Myst*, it required a fair amount of scholarship. (Which was what probably killed it in the marketplace). The goal of the game, as far as he knew, was to gather together all of the pieces of the Emerald Tablets of Hermes Trismegistus and arrange them in the proper order. The thing was, the tablets had been scattered all over the computer-landscape, in phrases, symbols and sometimes even single letters.

Hence the notebook, which was filled with reproduced symbols, doodles, and translations, to help decode the puzzle. One of the texts used frequently as a "game bible," was his father's book, *Mercurial Magick*. Codebreakers on obscure message boards referred to 'the Davies,' as in, "look it up in the Davies." Or MM, for the acronym-lovers.

(Thank god that Irene didn't find his father's book in his work bag!)

Even now, as he dried the dishes, he thought about the game, its dance about imagery and glyphs marching across the screen. Just for one moment—he felt like Byron had felt. He was, in his own way, chasing a god.

Later that evening he tried playing *Trismegistus* for only an hour—but he looked up three hours later. Irene was in bed. He lay next to her, and fell asleep, thinking of one of the glyphs that had been in the game, trying to remember where he'd seen it before.

It hovered before him, burned on the skin of the night. It was a kind of cursive V. It faded by degrees, from burning gold to cool green.

"...Forget..."

The voice was cool green, like the floating letter. It was Viola's voice. She stroked him gently. Her hands were feather-soft.

But his mind muttered; it wouldn't shut down. The V still hovered.

He remembered it from Dad's book. There had been a chart, full of...

"Shhh," she hushed him. A sound like the wind, rustling through trees. "Turn away from that, Simon." Her voice was the parched, raspy one of her last days in the hospital. He remembered when he'd taken her hand, just as she died. Her skin was clammy and smelled of the medicine that coursed through her veins. The grip was light and as she left her body, her hand fell out of his. He settled down on her bosom. But the V was still in the middle of the room, until it was joined by another shape—this one a Z with a squiggle on the end. And another splashed into existence, a circle with a triangle, followed by a capital A with kind of hat above it.

"Simon!" Her mother's whisper was fierce this time, almost a rebuke.

But the shapes kept on appearing, and he watched them, gold and silver and green, until they molded themselves onto a man who emerged out of the shadows. It was like he had been there all along, right next to the wardrobe. Simon couldn't see his face, or his eyes—just the glowing letters and the vague shape of his body. But he could feel the presence. It was heavy and brooding. The inscribed man's eyeless eyes captured him in their gaze. Simon felt like an insect being drowned in amber. He found he couldn't look away.

The inscribed man grew. He grew until his head grazed the ceiling. The glyphs glowed. A, V, Z...

His mother shrieked. She stopped stroking his head with those soft fingers, and rose. When did she get wings? And claws? She flew towards the inscribed man (shadow) and ripped at him. The inscribed man raised his arm. Viola tore the fabric of his skin—

And the symbols scattered like stars—

Simon woke up sweating.

Irene murmured something from the depths of sleep and turned over. He found he couldn't go back to sleep.

He got out of bed, and headed for the laptop.

Therefore will all obscurity flee from you.
> —*Trans from the Tabula Smaragdina (Emerald*
> *Tablets of Hermes Trismegistus)*

It is getting hard to concentrate. Things are losing definition. For instance: the creature he is mindlessly following. She used to be more fearsome, with blood-spattered wings and a terrifying visage. Her voice rent the air. She used to have a name. Now, the woman-part is fading, subsumed into the head of an eagle. He has lost his name, and his sense of self as well. The cypress forest, the the scent of oranges and asphodel washes over him in scent and sight. He almost loses himself in the gentle warm breeze that enrobes him. But some will, something stronger than the tides of death and forgetting urges him to follow the eagle that streaks through the air. It caws. *Come.*

So he follows. Through ancient forest, over hill and streams. Through settlements of the grey dead. (They all breathe their desolation like fine mist; their gazes are caught in the mist. He longs to join them. Not yet. Not yet.)

In the sky the eagle races against changes, from misty grey to vivid cobalt to tangerine honey. How long does he travel, endlessly, namelessly? But he knows the answer, maybe he's always known it. It was a name. Now, it is just a face, that of his son. The very least he can do now is save him from the obsession. The god-magician clouded his life, filled it with mystery and madness. The god-thief stole his soul away. The death-god led him here, to this grey land Will his son (name stolen from him, too) be trapped here, as well?

INSCRIBED

Of all strength this is true strength, because it will conquer all that is subtle, and penetrate all that is solid.

—Trans from the Tabula Smaragdina (Emerald Tablets of Hermes Trismegistus)

3:33 AM and Simon found the last fragment of the tablet. It made no sense, even translated from the glyphs. Some vague shit about the moon and the stars and the transformation of matter. In spite of everything, Simon felt close to Dad, finally. Oh, he'd never understand him completely, the path he chose. But he couldn't hate him anymore. A couple of mouse clicks, and the puzzle was solved. Maybe Byron was watching him But that was stupid. Or was it? He'd woken up to see some kind of man made of symbols, hovering over his bed, be attacked by his winged mother. He couldn't really make sense of that.

He solved the puzzle.

The screen went black.

Simon waited for the next phase. A liquid black crystal pause.

Then: Glyphs, alchemical symbols flew across the screen in all colors, from mint green to turquoise to silver grey. They swarmed like insects and and scattered like leaves. Gradually, the symbols settled, forming some kind of pattern. A pattern that Simon recognized—

He cursed. Of course.

"I knew it would be you," he said under his breath.

The Inscribed Man. The fucking thing that took Dad away from him and mom.

Was it worth it, Dad? Simon did not voice this. And yet the Inscribed Man on his computer reacted to something. Maybe it was just a part of the game's programming, but the man of symbols shivered and fell away. What materialized in its place was this:

A grey landscape, with distant mountains. In the foreground, cypress trees in grove. An old man stood before the altar that the emerald tablets rested on. The tablets themselves were shattered, into an emerald dust. The old man used a tree branch and smashed the remaining fragments into pulp. There were cuts on the old man's body, blood that he ignored

153

in his destructive frenzy.

Simon recognized the crazed, half naked man, even though he never looked up from his work.

"Oh, Dad."

Coalrose

She looks at them, imprisoned in a poster: a creamy sepia photo artfully blurred until the edges merge with the white borders. A cloud of frizzy hair shaped in a bun with her trademark 'do: two elegant, snaky strands to frame her high forehead. Her full lips are slightly parted, and her dark eyes glisten sensually. She's wearing a black velvet blouse embroidered with an Oriental design. A white lace skirt covers her booted feet in foam. At first glance it is simply a romantic '30s style photograph. But she changes, ever so slightly, like she's watching you. Sometimes, there's a tear in the corner of her eye, a tiny diamond of vulnerability. Other times, she is brutal and mocking: a sliver of tongue shows between the too-white teeth. And sometimes she is enticing – her blouse open slightly and you can see, nesting in her cleavage, the start of the legendary tattoo.

Here's a picture Zoë Coalrose nude. Hands hide her eyes. The fuzzy, out-of-focus room is bare. Skeletal. (The negative is in such bad shape...) All you see of her face is her lips, which are twisted. Is she crying? Or laughing? But she makes it clear that she is responding to the photographer.

I: Etta (1930)

Mama warned her of juke joints, with their zoot-suited criminals, peddling prostitution and cocaine. So she managed to steer clear of Harlem, somehow. This fear made her miss Lena Horne at the Apollo and Cab Calloway at the Cotton Club. But he stood in front of her now, in spite of her caution, a cigarette dangling from his teeth. His conked hair shone in the weak winter sunlight. His suit was ostentatiously white, his fedora arrogantly perched on his head. A hot pink handkerchief obscenely peeked out of his suit's pocket.

"Hey, gal," he said. His eyes slowly swept up and down her body, deliberately stopping at her breasts. "How you doin'."

Etta pulled her coat close against her as she decided how to deal with him. It was daytime, in the middle of a very busy 6th Avenue. Maybe she had nothing to worry about. She would play it straight.

"I am doing fine; and yourself, sir?"

Zoot Suit smiled widely. Lots of gold sparkled in his mouth. He would have been good-looking without them. But with them he was positively irresistible. "You from the South, huh? Whereabouts?"

"Just outside of Atlanta," Etta said. She started sweating, in spite of the cold. She could practically see into his mind. She saw a small, dirty fleabag room, with a green dresser-drawer. She saw herself and this man (Dewey was his name) snorting a trail of white powder he'd arranged on her nude body, then having his way with her. Violently. Etta gasped. The image was so real.

"Why you so jumpy?" Dewey asked her. (How did she know his name?)

"Because I've got to be on my way." And she made to move.

He grabbed her by the arm. "Where you got to be so fast, darlin'?"

She smelled his desire, rank beneath his super sweet perfume. Perfume stronger than her own (she wore vanilla extract, a cheap, country fragrance substitute).

"Please, sir." Etta looked around frantically. Throngs of indifferent New Yorkers wove through the sidewalks. None of them gave a damn about a colored girl. They probably thought Dewey – *how do I know his name?* – was her pimp. She suddenly wanted to be back in her home just outside of Atlanta, with its pastures, sweet water and hundreds of kind, loving faces.

"You ain't got nowhere to go, gal." Dewey was leering at her. She jerked herself out of his grasp. He grabbed her again.

Then he jumped back, and doubled over in pain. "Damn, gal! What the fuck you got in your purse? A lightening rod?..."

His voice was fading and distant, because Etta was walking away quickly. She was shaking, from all the violence she'd seen in his mind.

Mama was right. New York *was* a far cry from Atlanta. In Atlanta she was safe, the people in her neighborhood were friendly, completely unlike the folks in her tenement. Some were nice, but many of them had developed that callous rudeness that seemed so prevalent in the North.

Etta stopped in the middle of the street. She felt a little faint. She checked her watch: she still had time to spare. Enough for a cup of coffee, to get herself together. She entered Café Robincheau, and ordered a cup and a madeliene. Some of the patrons stared at her. She ignored them. *I have to develop a thicker skin, if I'm to make it here.* This was true. There was no self-contained community to support her like there was back home. The theater scene here was so insular. She had no desire to join the route of the tawdry showgirls that populated the Harlem stage. She wanted to be a serious actress. Last year, before she got the scholarship to Barnard, she had been the star of the Negro Dramatic Arts production of *A Midsummer Night's Dream.* She'd attracted the attention of several county newspapers. Etta sipped her sweet and bitter brew. She nibbled her cookie, gently flavored with a hint of lemon. The people in the café looked like extras in a Dickens novel, with bloodshot eyes and ruddy noses. A few glared at her. *Let them stare.* It was still a novelty, being able to go where you wanted to, even after all these months. Jim Crow was a presence in her, but he was slowly dying. She closed her eyes, erasing Dewey, his name, his face from her mind. Her mother's voice came up instead: "If you'd gone to Spellman, you wouldn't have had this problem..."

She laughed. The cruelty and the danger were all worth it to her. This city (*the* City) was fascinating, with its tempos, languages, smells and different kinds of people. Home was nice, but a little boring. She saw herself getting married to her first boyfriend, Terrence, and putting her dreams on a shelf somewhere, to collect dust. Living her mortal existence in an endless flurry of children, cooking, cleaning, and church. Beginning each conversation with, "I used to be an actress..." Etta wanted to be an immortal, forever on black vinyl, or on the Silver Screen. Not that she had any illusions about the roles available for colored actresses. Acting was her passion. She felt she could tap into other people's souls, and weave their feelings together. She gave them back to the people watching. Puck had been easy. Androgynous and ageless, s/he seemed to exist in a corner of everyone's mind. So Etta wove the rural haints, shades, and spirits of the audience into the English woodland fairy. It was like echoing, people's dreams and souls. She couldn't *not* do it, even if she tried. How she managed, she didn't question. It was a gift.

She had been Puck, lived his ephemerality. That had to count for something –

She glanced at the ornate clock on the café wall. Realizing the time, she finished her coffee and brought the rest of the cookie with her. It wouldn't do to be late for her first meeting with Harold.

Etta had met him when she posed for a Columbia University art class. The pay was terrible and the work boring. But it did give her some exposure to the art crowd. She figured that since she couldn't get a toehold in the theater community, she'd try the next best thing. (Maybe some casting director would be looking for a *type*)...

Harold looked like a weasel with dark, close eyes and sharp, rodent-like features. A few wisps of hair were on his chin, and angry red acne. He looked suspicious, but Etta didn't feel anything bad about him. She only saw his art. For some reason, images of brown women clad in bright, solid colors, in a lush tropical setting, danced around in his mind. A few weeks ago, Etta had gone to the Metropolitan Museum of Art and seen these very images for real. They got to talking, after the session, about Gaugin and other artists. Etta knew next to nothing about art. But she somehow knew what pieces he was talking about. They floated in the air. They became friends, of a sort. He took her out to dark, salon-like cafes, where she was introduced to espresso and biscotti. Places she could never go in Georgia. (If they even had places like these in Georgia). The names he dropped – Cocteau, his chance encounter with Gertrude Stein when he lived in Paris – she wasn't familiar with. After a conversation with him, however, she found that she knew the plot of *Les Enfants Terrible*, or knew of the burgeoning artist's community on the Left Bank. She put it down to his passion. When Harold spoke, spit charmingly flew everywhere, his eyes had a far away glimmer, like beetles' wings. And his acne – they were blood anemone decorations for his face. When he invited her to be a model in his new project, she'd been more than delighted.

Etta reached the building and rang the buzzer. It was a dilapidated building, the color of cigarette ash. He buzzed her in. Cat piss and broken marble. Grimy stairwells and squalling children. But there was something arty and mysterious about it. A romantic ruin. She came to a scraped door that had loud music blaring out of it. Count Basie.

Etta knocked demurely. She got no response. Her knocking became louder. Harold opened the door, disheveled. He was unshaven and smelled of beer. His acne seemed to ooze.

"Come in," he said indecorously. He motioned for her to sit in a chair littered with old clothes. He offered her a dirty glass of water before he went to his bedroom to get ready. Etta glanced around the exposed pipes, the greasy accordion radiator and the pock-marked floor. There was something not right about this. *Maybe I'm still shaken up about what happened earlier,* she thought.

Harold came back with a dirty, paint-spattered shirt and pants. "I'm ready," he grunted. "You sit there."

She meekly complied. This was deeply ingrained in her. Where she was from, if you looked at a white person the wrong way, it could mean death. But she was disturbed by his gruffness. She moved over to the makeshift throne he'd made of a wooden chair. Holey cushions, hard wood. An off-white tarp was draped behind her. She became acutely aware of the coldness of the room.

"Take off your clothes," said Harold.

She did as she was told. This was nothing new; she'd posed nude before. She gathered herself up in a proud pose. And she was proud: no matter what the outside world said, she thought her brown, glossy, muscled body was beautiful. For the next twenty minutes, she posed and preened. These were tasteful, arty photographs. Her religious mother might not understand, but that didn't matter. For most of the time she was able to shut out the dark thoughts that darted in Harold's mind. Then they changed. Etta could trace the change of the session to a glare in Harold's eye. The blood dots on his skin seemed to pulse.

"Spread your legs," he whispered. His urbanity, his education slipped from him. He was a pornographer. Somehow, she knew this: that he made and sold pornography to pay for his other art projects.

A shred of something made her say no.

He made her regret it.

"Now come on! Don't be like that." He'd raised his voice immediately. "Just relax," he softened his voice, "let the camera capture your – *essence*. No. No. If you think you're getting out of here without me getting what I want – "

She'd stood up. He approached her now, menacingly. She sat down. Jim Crow stirred and rose within her.

"Yes, that's right. Now spread those thighs. You're so pretty. Now come on! Put your hands down. *Relax*."

She had started crying. She wanted home, now. Fried chicken, lazy summer days, Mama's bosom warm and soft. Then she heard Harold's voice, his hidden voice: *Stupid nigger bitch, she's more trouble than she's worth. Who'd want to buy these pictures anyway? Who'd want to fuck a thing like that?*

That shred of something that she'd felt before stirred. It grew, like a fire. Rage. She took her face out of her hands, and looked at him, dead on, through her tears.

Harold was saying something; she'd better stop crying or else.

That acne on his face shone an unwholesome red color. Not like blood anemones at all. Nor like the comforting red clay of Georgia riverbeds that she'd played in when she was little. No. They were like ants, fire ants. A red swarm of fire ants on his face. His skin was pale, white like lime powder. Lime, that you sprinkle down an outhouse, to stop the stink and decompose the fecal matter. If you got lime on your hands, you'd better run to your Mama, before it starts burning. Fire ants, swarming over hills of white lime and dried river beds of red clay. Fire ants, devouring the red, red blood of anemones. Harold had been talking. Etta barely noticed when he stopped. She couldn't, however, miss him screaming. Or him clawing at his face, at his acne. Count

Basie's trumpeter drowned out the screams. They stopped before the record was over.

Etta stood up, looking at his body. It was still, even though his eyes were opened. There was no blood. No ants. What had she done?

I killed him. I wanted him dead, and now he is. She didn't need to feel his pulse. No thoughtforms swirled in his mind; that was knowledge enough. She gathered her things and began to dress. She did this mechanically. She felt – this emotion was new, and nameless. She felt soulless. *I know that I am evil now. The Lord can't help me. Dewey and Harold just recognized the evil within me. Dirt attracts dirt. Just 'cause I drew them, and their evil to me, does that mean that I should've killed them?* When she was dressed, she went to the Victrola and plunked the needle back down onto the phonograph recording. She did this listlessly, as if she were in some other's employ. Etta passed by Harold's inert form, ruined by her evil, and left. When she reached the outside, she glanced back. The building wavered and darkened. It whispered, *Who would want to fuck a thing like that?* Dewey's unctuous mind and flea-bitten bed. Harold's Paris and Gauguin, never to live again. His skin, bursting with pornographic flowers, ants writhing on their petals...

Etta turned and ran.

Another poster shows Zoë Coalrose as Venus, with whispery fabric gracefully dropping to the feather-strewn floor. Clam shells mask her forbidden parts, hair extensions cascade down her back as she leans against a pillar. She is not conventionally beautiful. She is much too dark, her nose is too wide and flared, her breasts and buttocks too voluptuous. Yet, if she is not a classical Venus, she is some darker aspect of Her. Love gone wrong, or unquenchable desire. Maybe closer to the earthy, pagan vision of the goddess.

II: Vivian (1931)

It was such an obvious pseudonym, Vivian had to laugh. It smacked of pretension and stood out on a roster full of Marys and Alices. He had to give it to the dancer, though. Anything to stand out.

He kept his voice neutral as he called out, "Zoë Coalrose." Maury, the show's producer sitting to his left, briefly glanced up from the pile of account books spread out before him. His assistant, Miss Clementine, was the very model of engagement.

A short, dark girl walked on stage. She was darker than a brown bag, and had wide hips. Coalrose, indeed. Her nose was flat, her lips too full. She wore an unflattering shade of pink. Poor thing—she probably didn't know the unspoken requirements for Negro performers. It would be a rude awakening. Viv looked over at Maury; there was a frown on his face. Maury hated auditions, and at the same time, he insisted on attending them. The Negro Follies was *his* show, and Maury felt he had to oversee every aspect of it.

"You can begin at anytime," he informed the dark girl. She nodded to George, who plonked out a workman-like version of "Some of These Days."

Viv settled in for a minute or two of a middling performance. He thought of a children's book he'd once seen, with a female hippo in a pink tutu, gracelessly pirouetting over a stage...

The stage gets brighter, the light intensifying. White light, Viv knows, is made up of an arcane combination of the color spectrum. Somehow, he can see how each strand of color, a ribbon of yellow, a slash of red, a flow of blue all come together, in illumination. They make and unmake the strand of light that comes from no spotlight on the dancing girl. The dark girl who whirls in pink, like an azalea blossom caught in honey...

Viv sat up, shook his head. It was too early to fall asleep. Sure, auditions were tedious affairs. But he prided himself on not drifting off, for having a strong focus. Viv looked at the stage, at the pathetic girl moving on the stage...

She is no longer a girl in a pink dress. She's no longer a she. She is darkness devouring pink, pink swallowing darkness. An evolving statute, form and formlessness coming together. The shapes she makes with her body are repulsive and mesmerizing. Snake and stone; sylph and sinner; air and angel. Evershifting...

Viv turned away from the stage. To focus on the Coalrose girl was to be nauseous. The things she did with rhythm and her body were... wrong. Instead, he watched Maury, anticipating his signal to end the audition. He was transfixed, his eyes glassy, his mouth slightly open. Mouthbreathing. Viv looked at Miss Clementine—the same look was frozen on her face. Viv turned to the stage, to the spinning form in front of him. He intended to pause the audition, and suggest that she try one of signature dances of the show, the Can Can. Before he could open his mouth, the music changed to boogie-woogie, and Coalrose was swiveling her hips and buttocks like Josephine Baker. The light divided into gay and merry colors, swirls of lemon and cobalt. Viv couldn't look away—he was ensnared. The dark, heavy girl danced the universe into creation on the stage. Viv knew the universe would stop when she stopped dancing.

III: Bertram (1933)

I was closing up shop when the colored woman came in. She was short, not more than five feet if an inch, but for all that, she was uppity. She strutted in my store like a prize rooster.

"Ma'am," I said as nice I as could, "We're closing. And 'sides, we don't tend to your sort."

I indicated the sign on the wall: MUST WEAR SHOES. NO DRUNKS. NO WOMEN. NO COLOREDS. I didn't want no trouble, but she didn't move an inch. Maybe she couldn't read. She didn't look drunk, but she was certainly a woman and a nigra. She said, in a high falutin voice, "I would like a tattoo, and I understand that you are the best."

"Why thank you. Much obliged. But as I said...I can't help you. Maybe there's a colored tattoo artist somewhere. I don't know. But I can. Not. Help. You." I moved toward her, put my hand on her arm, with the intention of steering her toward the door. But she wouldn't budge. She was a statue, a complete dead weight. It was like she weighed a thousand pounds. And she smiled at me. It was like – I swear – almost a pitying look, as if she was sorry about something. Now, I know from experience that ladies can fight something fierce. Neath their dresses, makeup and high heels many a woman is a wild cat, just waiting to come to life.

She said, soft and dangerous, "Please."

I said, firm and threatening, "No." I could get in trouble for working on a nigger. Word gets around fast, and I'm not saying I agree with it, but some folks won't patronize an establishment that works on their kind.

Now, I don't have the words to describe what happened next, but I'll try. I have my beliefs. I never saw a ghost or a flying saucer or anything like that, but I can't say they don't exist, cause who knows? I've seen good buddies, real sensible ones who could face death and disease and famine reduced to tears because they saw something they couldn't explain, the face of a long dead relative in a window, or the Blessed Virgin speaking to them while they were ill. I believe in Good, and I believe in Evil. Angels and demons, that sort of thing. (You can't travel around the world like I have and *not* believe in it; there are things in the East that will convince you of deviltry). I also believe that there are things that can't really be explained in those two categories. Forces of nature...

I'm not an artist. At least, I don't think what I do is art. Mother's names, crosses, skulls, dancing mermaids, the occasional more elaborate thing, like the Chinese dragon I once inked on a young man's skin. But sometimes, I get inspired. I've had a couple of fellas come in here, and told me to draw whatever I wanted. And once I was certain they wasn't drunk, I've done it. Mostly abstract stuff, patterns and the like. So when the colored gal sat down on the chair, and bought out her breast, I got one of those inspirations. It was immediate. I didn't have no choice. That curve of brown flesh told me what it wanted on it. The vision came silently, slithering. Vines, thorns and the curled blossoms of burnt roses. I know that I'd do the job, or it would bother me, somehow. Like those dark roses would carve themselves into my brain like a medieval woodcut. I don't remember getting my instruments. They just appeared, plucked from the bright darkness in my shop. I don't remember tracing the design on her brown flesh. Black ink flowed under her skin, while a thin trickle of blood rose from her, like an exchange of fluids. I was worried that the detailed work I was doing would fade, because her skin was so dark. But each rose, each thorn, each vine was defined, with a living blackness that I've spent many an hour trying to recreate. Black is all colors, right? Even when I mixed my most vivid inks together, it only looks gray beneath lily-white skin. How was I able to get that color on Negro skin?

When I was finished, there was a spray of black roses on her breast, hiding in a thicket of thorns.

As I put the gauze over the new tattoo, she said, "Now, was that so bad?"

She rose from the chair like she was a queen. She left a wad of bills on seat, and floated out into the predawn light.

I closed up and walked to Eli's Diner to get a cup of joe. And I saw her again, her face staring at me from a poster. THE NEGRO FOLLIES AT THE CHTHONIAN, the poster said in bright red lettering. Beneath the arc of words, ('One Week Only!') there were drawings of spooks dancing, and at the center, there was a great, fat lady spook with feathers coming from her hair. Though it was a caricature, I'd recognize that face anywhere. In smaller, black letters, the poster read, 'Featuring the Exotic Zoë Coalrose.' Don't know why, but I shivered, remembering the lost hours, filled with black roses and prickly vines. I swear, I thought I saw 'em begin to spill out of the poster, like tiny black ants.

Zoë made her appearance at the Panther Club in Chicago. See the publicity still from one of her acts. Her hair is short and in a Marcel wave. She stares at the camera and not even the ghost of weakness is there. She wears a translucent gown; more of a robe, really. On her breast, there peeks out the tattoo: a rose, its thorny vine begins to trail down into her cleavage. A rose that's a threat. Zoë eventually became a headliner at the Panther Club. She was called the Josephine Baker of the Midwest. I've got a picture of it. Even in black and white, it's a glittering ornament. Colson's book *Erotomania* describes the Panther Club like this:

"The front of the Panther Club was shaped like the onion part of a minaret, done in black marble. A flight of black marble stairs led to the circular doorway, guarded by two stone panthers. A large, neon pink sign flashed in front, in Arabic stylized letters. Inside was a scene from the 1001 Nights. The waiters were dressed in turbans with costume jewelry and fiery garments. Palm trees lined the walls, and instead of seats, there were cushions. Men would sit down, order exotic drinks, and the show would begin... It could be Angel, the blonde child-woman dressed as her namesake that they were looking for...or Jasmine, the belly dancer. Or it could be Zoë, the smoldering, dancing temptress..."

Her dancing became legendary. She didn't do striptease like her colleagues. She refused. She put her heart into her movements. Against bright jazz, she would whirl and high-kick herself into a frenzy. By all accounts, it was spellbinding. Much more meaningful than the bump-and-grind such establishments were known for. But this was not mere entertainment for those who saw her. Her power to weave and shape the stuff in minds was still there.

IV: Lenora (1935)

The junk in her veins didn't send her anymore. So when they came inside her mouth or her vagina, she felt it, and heard their grunting. But sometimes, if Lenora closed her eyes as they were kissing or fondling her, she could see something else. Or someone else. As rough and unshaven as their faces could be, as stinking with whiskey and gin as their breath was, if she worked hard enough, Lenora could see *her*. That dancer's soft mouth, pressed against hers. The dancer's hands, exploring her body. But this never lasted. For one thing, johns were always crude. They couldn't help that. And for another, males were invasive.

The junk didn't work.

This man grunted. Through her hurt, she was cool. Pressed against his chest, she didn't know or care if he was black or white, married or not. (So, in one way, the junk *did* work). She merely noticed that he was being transported. She wasn't. After he finished, he slapped money down on her dresser, and went into the bathroom. Lenora showed him out of the door. As she walked to her bed, she passed the mirror. She looked at herself analytically. How old was she now? She forgot sometimes. She was nineteen. Her breasts sagged, her neck was covered in bites from overexcited men, her arms with track marks. She looked like she was forty. Good. Maybe she wouldn't have to do this work anymore. She'd have a real reason to quit. Except how could she afford her need?

Lenora didn't really care much. She would find a way. And if she died of hunger for this stuff, so be it. Some hungers are better to die of than others.

She walked over to her dresser, collected the money, still greasy with his essence, and put it in her purse. She set about getting dressed. She rifled through her closet, throwing on the first dress that she touched. She was on her way out when the mirror caught her attention again. The dress. Royal blue, with tiny white daisies printed on it. Camilla's dress. She couldn't wear it.

Before she knew it, Lenora was fighting with the dress, wrestling to get it off. It seemed to take a while. Finally, it was a blue ball of daisies in a corner of the room. Lenora went to her closet again with a vengeance. Finding a pair of slacks and a blouse, she forced herself into them. Which wasn't hard to do, considering that there wasn't much of her to shove into anything.

As she left her tiny room, she kicked at the balled up dress. At Camilla.

It really is all her fault, Lenora thought as she bolted down three flights of stairs. She wouldn't be like this, living like this, if it weren't for Camilla. Dusk was settling in on the streets as she made her way to the grocery store. She would buy some food. The leftover money would buy her junk and some needles from Brand.

Three years ago she had lived a pretty good life in Hickory, North Carolina. Papa was a preacher, Mama was a seamstress. The white house with green shingles had always been filled with love, God and the congregation's gifts of food. Collard greens and chitterlings perfumed the place, seemed to emanate from the very wallpaper. The living room was mostly full of Mama's sewing things: headless female torsos and wooden body frames draped with fabrics, or stuck with pins. It was the mannequins that first tipped her off, that she might be different. There was something about their forms. The gentle slopes, curves and swells of their bodies spoke of grace. It wasn't that men's bodies were bad – she didn't feel that *then*, at least – it was just that they didn't call to her in the same way. Nothing echoed there. But Lenora ignored this feeling. God was a god of brimstone, judgment, and distance. Eventually she would marry a man and bear children.

But the feeling, this difference, didn't go away. When she played spin-the-bottle with the boys at birthday parties, she felt their wet lips on her skin, her mouth. But no connection. Maybe that would change in time. Lenora immersed herself into sports. She became something of a star on the girls' softball team. In the ninth grade she'd even won a trophy. But the accolades of her school, the rigors of the game, the trips to Greensboro, Gastonia, and Durham, these did nothing to fill the hollow space inside of her. There was nothing to cool the hot space she felt inside when she saw the girls' sweaty bodies, their muscles and breasts straining against grimy uniforms. After games, in the showers, taking furtive glances at slick forms underneath the water sprays. One girl from an away team caught her looking once. She smiled back.

Her name was Joanna. They became friends. They talked about softball, college and future plans. But not boys. This went on for about a week. At the end of the week, underneath Joanna's school's bleachers, they kissed. Lenora thought at first that she was going to Hell. But the feeling she felt when they kissed, it was how she imagined people felt when they were filled with the Lord. In Papa's congregation, when someone felt the Holy Ghost's presence, they would flop around like fishes, or slither like serpents on the church's floor. In Joanna's arms, she'd gasp for air and slither over her body. Surely this was just another way to get the Spirit, wasn't it? And if it wasn't, did God want her to feel hollow and empty the rest of her life?

One day, when she was sure that Mama and Papa would both be out of the house on various business, she invited Joanna over. They were pretty far along when Mama opened the door to Lenora's room. It seemed that she'd left something or other in there, maybe her good shearing scissors. It happened so fast.

With junk clouding her mind, Lenora could only remember bits and pieces. Mama fainting, Joanna leaving. Shivering and naked on the bed. Mama and Papa conferring. Papa, his black skin purpled from the rage coloring his face, quoting Bible verses: Corinthians 6: 9-10. No, not quoting; *screaming*.

Lenora shook her head. Junk could do that sometimes, cloud the brain. That, or the need of junk. She passed by a wall plastered with posters of *her*. Zoë Coalrose. Her bright smile shone from her dark face. Lenora found it irresistible. A few weeks ago she'd even stole one of the posters from this wall. It lay on her closet floor. There was something enchanting about the features. Something she couldn't place. She wasn't beautiful. But she was. The tawdry showgirl dress showed her cleavage. The black rose tattoo hid there. Lenora loved the name, too. It was poetic, and it was also funny. That ugly girl with a weird, hypnotic quality was something this Coalrose character had in common with Camilla, her only real lover.

For someone sixteen and just recently kicked out of her house, Lenora showed a remarkable resilience. For two nights she slept in the park near her home. On the third day, she watched and waited for her folks to leave the white house with green shingles. When they had, she broke in, smashing a window and went to the coffee can where the emergency money was kept. With two hundred dollars in hand and a suitcase of clothes (including some of the clothes that Mama intended to give to paying customers), Lenora walked to the bus station and bought herself a ticket North, to Chicago. After two days of cramped quarters and bad greasy spoons she arrived in the Windy City, exhausted. Somehow she found a women's hotel for that night. A few days later she found a job at Madsen's Funeral Parlor.

It was a stroke of luck. She walked in amidst the wax flowers, polished coffins, thinking that she was going to see an embalmed corpse and lose what little lunch she'd eaten before. It turned out that Mr. Madsen was from North Carolina, too. He'd migrated to the North years ago after finishing his mortician's degree.

"There's good money in death," he'd told her.

He was an elegant and dour man, without the slightest trace of a Southern accent. With an uncharacteristic wink he said, "Of course I'll help a hometown girl out. Even if you aren't from my hometown proper." She became his receptionist.

Madsen's Funeral Parlor was a family-owned and run business. Mrs. Madsen handled the books. She, like her husband, was serious, her "good" hair always wound up in tight, severe bun. And like her husband, she had a warm streak like a vein of gold hidden within rock. Their daughter Camilla arranged the presentation of the funeral services. Flower and candle arrangements were her domain. That was about all she could handle.

Where her parents were stern and serious, Camilla was blushingly silly. Where they were warm and genuine, she was sweet and distracted. She was the color of caramel candy with soft, brown hair and large, shining dark eyes. Her plumpness and thick, lustrous lashes added to her charm. Camilla took to Lenora like a bee to honey.

At first, Lenora thought that this was merely annoying. She was cloying, both in her personality and the toilet water she drenched herself in. She would talk to Lenora as if she were a character in those awful girlie novels that she hated. One day after Friday dinner at the Madsen's, the two of them had gone to Camilla's bedroom – a nightmare of dollies, doilies and chintz – ostensibly to check out dress patterns. Lenora had sat on the frilly, frou-frou bedspread, plotting her escape when Camilla shyly clutched her hand. Lenora thought that she was going to go into one of her "we're the best of friends, ever" speeches. It was a shock when Lenora learned of her true intentions. For a year and a half the two became secret lovers. Eventually they moved in together in an apartment subsidized by the oblivious Madsens.

For that time Lenora was her life-sized dress-up dolly, cook and maid. Lenora was reasonably happy; what more could a black lesbian without a diploma ask for? It wasn't her lot to question things. Then Camilla decided to get married. The not-so-oblivious Madsens found a suitable beau from one of Chicago's burgeoning black bourgeois families. Camilla didn't protest; maybe she couldn't. The ever warm-hearted Madsens told her that she could still live in the nice, dollhouse apartment, for a low rent. Lenora refused. She had her pride...

The grocery store was coming up quickly. She shook the fog out of her head and tried to concentrate on what she needed. Some kind of fruit, apples maybe. Some kind of meat... She teetered a bit. She almost bumped into the flower stall in front of the store. The little Asian man who ran the cart looked perturbed.

"Look, man, I'm sorry; I ain't mean to do that..." She was unsure if she'd spoken aloud or not.

Flowers. Girlie things. Camilla loved them. They looked like candy-colored lace skirts to her. Except – there, on one of the shelves, there was a bouquet of black roses. She'd never seen any roses that color before. The color of ink. *Coalroses.* Something, she didn't know what, made her buy six of them. The Asian man called them Midnight roses. She blew her food money; so what? She walked further on, not knowing what to do with the roses. *Maybe I'll build some sort of shrine or something, with the poster and the roses... I wonder if she's seen them, these coal-roses. I bet she has*—Lenora had an idea. It was crazy, but she couldn't stop herself. Before she knew it she was on a bus headed for the Westside.

It was only until she got to the door the club that she recognized that absurdity of what she was about to do. They probably wouldn't let her in. She could hear them now: *Fuckin' bulldagger wants to see the Panther Club...* No, this was a bad idea. The junk's idea. A waste of money, another hungry night. She held the midnight roses and began to walk away from the gaudy, ornamented club. Just then a shiny black Cadillac pulled up. A liveried driver got and opened the back door. Zoë

Coalrose stepped out.

Her ebony flesh was encased in a spangled, brilliant strapless dress. She seemed to drift. She floated to the stairs of the club.

"Miss Coalrose – "

They tried to stop Lenora, a group of men.

But, "It's alright, fellas," came the dusky contralto. Dusky and dulcet at once. They parted to let the little junkie girl who could've been forty hand her a bunch of black roses. Coalrose smiled, and her smile was brighter than her dress. It reminded Lenora of diamonds, even though she knew that this was impossible. It was a smile of welcome.

"What you got for me, sugar?" Zoë asked her.

Lenora felt as silly as Camilla as she gave her the bouquet.

"Ain't you sweet," said the dancer, accepting them, "coal-roses."

Lenora caught a glimpse of the tattoo, the thorny vines winding down her cleavage.

Zoë handed the flowers to an attendant bodyguard. "Would you like my autograph?" she asked her. The two coils on her forehead seemed to move. Being wrapped in their tendrils wouldn't be so bad...

"I don't have anything for you to sign, Miss Coalrose; I just wanted..." *Stupid fool,* she thought, *I'm crying...*

"Come here, sugar," said Coalrose. She embraced her. She kissed her forehead, and knew. Her father, God, the mannequins, Camilla, her first hit of heroin, hooking, everything. And in turn Lenora knew about her: a frightened girl named Etta, running and hiding from herself and the evil that was lurking in her mind. The evil subsuming the Southern girl, and the birth of Zoë. The coils on Coalrose's head were rose vines. The thorns pierced her. Something soothing and cold spread throughout her body. This contact which seemed to last for a long time was over.

"See you later, darlin'," said Coalrose. She began ascend the steps. "Take care of yourself, sweet thing." She disappeared behind the doors of club.

The sweet chill in her body rejuvenated her. The whispering of the stuff in veins died down. She didn't feel quite so old. But Lenora *was* hungry. She found a diner not far from the Panther Club, and ate a large breakfast. Pancakes, bacon, coffee and orange juice – it never tasted so good. It gave her energy. It was night when she emerged from the diner. She took the L back to her dingy little apartment. It would be all right, somehow. *For Christsakes, I'm running!* Her veins sang. They were free. The gaunt, ugly men would never touch her body again.

"Nora!" Someone called her name. She was underneath the clattering platform of the L. She saw Brand, her dealer, not far from where she was. He was walking quickly towards her.

"Nora, let's you and me have conversation. I got something you're gonna like…"

"No, I'm busy right now."

"Some fella can wait a few minutes to get off. Lemme show you something – "

"No!" He'd been guiding her to an alley near the elevated tracks. "Let me go!"

He stopped. In the darkness, she could sense him sizing her up. She moved toward the streetlights. He followed.

"Well," he said slowly, "what have we here? What's gotten into you?"

"I don't need your stuff anymore. I don't need it."

"The hell you don't." He laughed.

And Lenora looked at him. *Looked* at him. Brand looked straight back at her. The thorns that had pierced her grew, and slithered. She could feel them rising behind her eyes. Roses. They rustled, kind of making her eyes itch a little. The vein-vines glowed with darkness. Her own darkness.

Brand backed down. He must've seen them, a silent garden of coalroses in her eyes, daring him. His voice cracked as he said, "Don't know what the fuck's gotten into you… but you'll be back…" He backed away, uncertainly.

When she got to her apartment, Lenora turned on the light. It was just a hunch, as she walked to the mirror. Her face was the face of a nineteen year old. Her skin was new. It glowed.

V: Victor (1962)

The Vine was run down. The red vinyl of the banquettes were more maroon, and the flocked wallpaper held cigarette smoke and stains. An old Chinese waiter, his face as pebbled as a beach, led me to my table, to the left of the stage. A candle flickered in a red fishbowl, illuminated nothing. Since I really didn't drink, I ordered Simon's favorite—a gimlet. The drink appeared before me—it was too dark too see beyond the gloom of the club—and I sipped the harsh lime infused concoction. "For you," I whispered, and toasted the empty seat.

I looked at the dingy stage. A double bass rested against a stand, and a piano was angled to the side. A microphone, a silver plant with a mechanical flower at its top, stood between the two instruments. So, she was going to sing. Not surprising—she was a bit long in the tooth to be dancing. I didn't like her voice. In fact, I didn't think she could really sing. Hers was a quivering contralto, full of drama. There were times when she didn't sing at all—she just spoke the words. The only thing I did like about her 'music' was that the repertoire was a little unorthodox. She eschewed the standards, your Basies and Gershwins, opting, instead, for things like lieder, chanson or folk songs along with the expected show tunes and gospel. "Too bad she has no talent," I'd say. Her records were dreary things, perfect for fog bound days in this damned city. Simon loved it, though. He was a complete devotee of Zoë Coalrose.

Her face stared down at us from the framed poster he had in our living room. Her eyes followed you everywhere. And that odd tattoo that poked above from her cleavage... It was downright scandalous. I could only imagine what Mother would say if she saw it. (As if she ever would travel across country to visit her homophile son). Yes, there was something sinister about the poster. But it had been his prized possession. I couldn't bear to remove it, after he passed away.

"She gives me strength," he told me once, during one of our fights. When he was bedridden, I moved the poster into bedroom so that she could look down on him as he slept. When I did that, I could swear his nightmares disappeared, and the fevers were no longer as fierce. Nevertheless, the poster creeped me out. I remember one vivid nightmare: her nude body with pendulous breasts, writhed in black roses. She was winged and vampiristic, as she drained the fever from sleeping Simon. The black roses got engorged, and burst, like boils. She was a comfort to Simon, yes. But ultimately, she couldn't save him. Maybe she leeched his life away....

That was a silly thought. I focused on the gimlet, its acidic sourness, the astringency of the gin.

"You're such a good boy," he'd say, when he drank and I stuck to Coca Cola or juice.

"Mama raised me right."

"Maybe I would've been raised right, if I had a Mama."

"What's the use of having a Mama," I'd say back, "if she won't talk to you?"

I knew that Simon had a past that he didn't talk much about. He'd been raised in various state institutions and by reluctant relatives. He drank too much, so his morning breath had that faint stink. He didn't age well at all—crows feet, washed out blond hair with a receding hair line, not-blue, not-green eyes caught in a web of burst capillaries. He was too loud and loved 'queening it up,' something that caused more than its fair share of trouble in public. But for all that, I missed him. I would give anything just to fight with him once more. Maybe that was why I was here.

Zoë Coalrose was a piece of Simon. Since he was gone, she would have to do.

The lights dimmed, with a single spotlight focusing on the mic. A pianist and a bassist walked out in the gloaming, while a man in a tailored tux stood in front of the microphone. He uttered some introductory words about the "legendary songstress and dancer" Coalrose as the duo played soft contemplative music. This theme continued until she took the stage herself.

She was shorter than I imagined, and had a matronly girth. But her hairstyle hadn't changed at all, the two snaky tendrils plastered to her forehead. A black velvet blouse with an Oriental design, the seafoam of lace swirled about her in a skirt. The black rose vine growing from her skin.

Coalrose started singing, and the room dropped into darkness. Her voice sounded ancient. Cigarettes, booze, years of screeching couldn't create that sound. It was the voice of a dying woman, scratchy and ravaged. She croaked out a tune, some piece from an old Broadway show long forgotten, and a song by Edith Piaf. The band played beautifully, deep bass tones, silvery piano notes that floated in the air. I still didn't like her voice, but it had a certain—charm? Gravitas? I couldn't place the word. She didn't really sing, per se. She *incanted* the words, gave them reverence, like a poetess. She made sure each break and quiver in her voice had a musical resonance. I was thrown back to when I first met Simon. Both of us were hayseeds from the sticks, and had joined the Navy. Neither of us had been further west than the Mississippi. He was tall, dashing and blond. I was small and black. Both of us were freaks. When we figured out the feelings between us, there had been hell to pay. But it was worth it. Both of us chose this fogbound city, far away from anyone we knew, at the edge of the world. Listening to Coalrose took me back to those endless Sunday nights, when mist walked the hills of the city and we were safe inside, listening to a dark voice as it curled through the night and Simon's cigarette rings...The flow of a white skirt. And I remembered as Zoë Coalrose watched over us. Her eyes following us everywhere. Black Madonna or vampire woman? As each song ended, the audience clapped thoughtfully. I was surprised that the room had filled up, and the number of folks in the audience. Mostly colored, a few whites scattered here and there. Her audience grew in darkness.

At the end of the set, Coalrose stopped to introduce her band in that deep, crackly voice. After that, she said, "I was born Etta Mae. Naïve, callow Etta, afraid of her own power. When she found what she could do, she died, and Zoë rose in her place. This song is dedicated to Etta."

I recognized the song within the first few notes played by the pianist. Everyone else did, as well—there was the gasp of recognition. This was Simon's favorite song. And Coalrose actually *sang* this one.

Years dropped off her vocal cords, and spoken words soared. But

I don't remember anything else about the performance. Because, I saw Etta, gingham dress, church hat and all, standing on the stage. Or— superimposed over the aged woman. But she faded as the song changed. She moved her hands and I swear, the spotlights and the shadow obeyed her.

It's masterful, isn't it?

I turned, and there was Simon. Or some part of him. Made of shadow and light, slithering with tendrils. His eyes were petals. I glanced around the room, to see if other people saw him. But everyone else had a flowered shadow around them. I glanced at my gimlet.

You aren't drunk. His shape rustled in time to the bass, the piano and voice. *I hear her everyday. In heaven.*

"Then you must be in the other place," I whispered to my man of shadow.

He laughed. Or rustled. And faded, as the song ended.

She didn't come out for an encore.

A stylish sister, dressed in a man's suit, quietly put a rose on the stage where Coalrose had stood.

Of course, it was black.

It took me years, but I found their stories, those touched by Zoë Coalrose. I'm sure that there are many others. I wasn't a fan, but I became one.

What she was, I don't know. There are words, but they are inadequate. But I think the clue is in her name. It's a work of genius, really. Zoë: an ancient name, evocative, resonant with power and nobility. It also sounds modern, as well. A tinge of the masculine in its pronunciation. And Coalrose. Coal is a nascent, unborn diamond, pure black that transforms into something that's clear, beautiful and unbreakable. A rose made of coal: intricate, kissed with the memory of fire.

About the Author

CRAIG LAURANCE GIDNEY's fiction has been a finalist for the Lambda Literary and the Gaylactic Spectrum awards.

He is the author of a collection *Sea, Swallow Me & Other Stories* and *Bereft*, a contemporary novel about bullying and racism. His website is craiglaurancegidney.com. Follow him on Twitter @ethereallad.

CPSIA information can be obtained
at www.ICGtesting.com
Printed in the USA
LVOW11s1550170118
563087LV00002B/185/P